CYNTHIA HICKEY

The Rancher's Dilemma

Book 1 in Finding Love in Disaster Series

CYNTHIA HICKEY

Written by: Cynthia Hickey
Published by: Winged Publications
Cover Design: Cynthia Hickey

This book is a work of fiction. Names, characters, places, and incidents are the product of the author's imagination and are used fictitiously. Any resemblance to actual events, locales, or persons, living or dead, is coincidental.

No part of this book may be copied or distributed without the author's consent.

Copyright © 2014 Cynthia Hickey
All rights reserved.

ISBN-13: 979-8-8690-8017-2

DEDICATION

To Tom, my one true love

ACKNOWLEDGMENTS

To Jan A, for her wonderful edits, and to all my readers who can't wait for the next new thing from me..

- **Ruth 2:10 NIV**

At this, she bowed down with her face to the ground. She exclaimed, "Why have I found such favor in your eyes that you notice me--a foreigner?"

CYNTHIA HICKEY

1

Kauai, Hawaii 1924

Lucy Dillow lay on her narrow bed, listening to the waves crash against the beach and tried to figure out what had woken her before the sun was fully risen. She swung her legs off the side of the bed. A slight vibration tickled her feet. Another tremor. She sighed. They were becoming all too familiar.

The aroma of frying sausage and sweet bread greeted her as she padded out of her room and into the small kitchen nook. "Good morning, Mama." She planted a kiss on her mother's cheek.

Mama took one glance at her bare feet and frowned. "You know I don't like you walking around like one of the natives."

"I just woke up. Did you feel the quake?" Lucy snatched a piece of sausage out of the pan, tossing it into her mouth before it burned her fingers.

"Who didn't? It seems as if they arrive every morning."

"And throughout the day." Lucy moved to the window. The sight of the ocean and the scent of the salt-filled breeze greeted her every morning. "I'd like to take a walk up to the volcano and see what's going on."

"Too dangerous." Mama handed her a plate. "You've work to do and students to teach. Your father is already out visiting those we minister to. You mustn't shirk your duties."

Lucy quickly ate before shoving her feet into the simple leather shoes her mother relented on letting her wear. If she had her choice, she'd run barefoot all day like the children she taught. After securing her hair in a bun and dressing in a simple navy skirt and white blouse, she grabbed her bag of teaching materials and headed out the door. She didn't have far to go. The tiny one-room schoolhouse was next door. Even at work, she couldn't get far from the demanding eye of Mama.

Pasting a smile on her face, she stepped into the school and wrote the day's vocabulary words, in English, on the board. When she realized she was writing words that had to do with love and romance, she started over. Finished, she wiped the chalk off her hands and stood in the doorway, ready to greet her students. Romance wasn't something she would find on the island. Not as a foreigner, anyway.

A man on a large red horse rode by. The sun cast highlights of blue on his black hair. His dark eyes were friendly as he gave her a nod. That was the type of man she wanted to marry someday. A strong man, a paniolo, a cowboy, but unfortunately, he looked like a native, and the natives didn't marry haole's, foreigners. She tossed him a smile and withdrew into the shadows of the schoolroom.

God had a husband for her, surely. All she needed to do was keep the faith and keep her eyes open. Her future could very well land in her lap. She might miss it if she wasn't paying attention.

She glanced at the gradual rise of land to her right. Smoke billowed from the crater of the Kilauea Volcano. Nothing new. The crater was always smoking, but the sky looked darker that morning.

A military jeep from Fort DeRussy rumbled past with several civilians as passengers. They drove toward the plume of smoke. Geologists? No matter about Mama's warning, Lucy was going to the crater when school ended that day. She wanted to see for herself whether there was anything to be concerned about.

Her twelve students arrived, all around the age of eight, sporting smiles and fresh-washed faces. "Aloha," she greeted. "Welcome." In order to teach all the children who needed her, she taught different ages in the morning and afternoon and on alternate days of the week. The small building wasn't big enough for more bodies at one time.

The children took their seats and pulled out their slates and chalk to write down the vocabulary words. They spent the next hour going over the words and their meanings in English. The students soaked up her teaching like suntanned sponges.

By the end of the day, exhaustion rested on Lucy's shoulders like a wet woolen shawl. Still, she hadn't changed her mind about visiting the volcano. She set her bag of supplies in her bedroom, grabbed her boots which were sturdier than the slippers she wore, and snuck past her mother cooking in the kitchen.

Outside, she removed her shoes and started the long walk up the road toward Kilauea. Another military truck rattled by, the soldier giving a friendly honk on his horn before stopping beside her. "Can I give you a ride?"

"No, thank you. It's a lovely day to walk."

"If you're heading to the volcano, it's quite a hike."

"I am, and I'll be fine."

He roared away, covering Lucy in a thin layer of volcanic dust. She brushed at her skirt and continued toward her destination. Dirt washed off easily enough, there was no cause to be offended by his leaving so quickly. He hadn't meant her any harm.

She lifted her face to the late afternoon sun. Life on the island was good, peaceful. There was no other place she ever wanted to live, although a short visit to the mainland wouldn't be a bad idea. She could replenish her school supplies and keep up on current worldly events. She sighed. Mama and Papa would never allow such a trip. Not alone, anyway. And, if Lucy were to go, they'd most likely ask her to stay there.

The air began smelling acrid the closer she got to the crater and pebbles littered the ground. She stopped to put her boots back on. By now, a crowd had gathered on the road, all heading toward the towering smoke. Behind them, rode the man Lucy had spotted that morning. He had donned a black cowboy hat to shade his face and made an imposing figure as he made his way to the top of the hill. He reminded Lucy of a general riding behind his army.

She smiled at her silliness and finished lacing her boots. Hiking her skirts, she dashed after the crowd.

Several men converged at the crater's mouth, arm movements and body language signifying they were in deep discussion. They stopped talking when Lucy approached.

She stepped forward and peered into the crater, the heat forcing her to step back. "What happened to the lava?"

"That's what we want to know, little lady." An older gentleman smoothed his mustache. "We're geologists here to find out what happened. Step back, now."

"The seismic activity has been increasing the last few weeks," the cowboy said, tilting his hat back. "While she's always expressed herself with smoke and fire, the ground shakes several times a day. Those rocks," he pointed to a couple of fist-sized rocks. "weren't there yesterday."

"Now, Mr. Garrison, it's quite possible somebody put those rocks there," the geologist said. "Let's not jump to conclusions. These tourists are always picking up something as a souvenir."

"I'm not jumping to anything, Mr. Woodward. This island is my home. I know this mountain. Don't discount my observations." Mr. Garrison stiffened. "Are we in danger of an eruption or not?"

"It's too soon to tell. "We'll know in a few days, after we do some tests." Mr. Woodward slapped a hat on his head and pushed his way through the crowd.

Lucy dashed forward. "Mr. Garrison, please tell me what you know."

"You heard the man. We don't know anything." His dark eyes narrowed. "You shouldn't be here. It's dangerous." He turned and marched away.

"I have as much of a right to know what is going on as you do." She ran to catch up with him. "Are you sure the rocks came from the volcano?"

"Yes. I've come here every day since April first." He swung into his saddle. "Go home, Miss—"

"Dillow. Lucy Dillow."

"The missionary's daughter?"

"Yes. Why?"

"I've heard about you. The keiki love you."

Her heart swelled. She knew the students enjoyed school, but to know they were talking about her filled her heart with joy. "As I do them."

"Good. Stay away from the danger up here and focus on your teaching."

She gasped and stomped her foot as he rode away. What an arrogant man. Focus on her teaching indeed!

~

Jack rode away from the volcano with a smile on his face. He'd made quite the impression on Miss Dillow. Stubborn girl. Why was she concerned about the volcano? Wasn't she busy enough with her teaching? An active geological site was no place for a young woman.

He didn't have time for missionaries and the

way they wanted to immerse themselves into everyone's lives. Teach the gospel to those willing to listen, school the young, and leave the rest of the islanders alone. That was his philosophy.

With the occasional glance over his shoulder at the plume of smoke and ash that grew taller daily, he made his way to his ranch and handed his horse to a stable boy. He rubbed his boots on a patch of tall grass before entering the house. Aneke, his cook and housekeeper, would tan his hide if he dirtied her floors.

He sniffed, the tantalizing aroma of grilled marlin greeting him. Aneke was the best cook he'd ever known. His stomach rumbled in response.

"Is that my Jack?" She'd called him that ever since his parents and fiancé died in a boating accident almost ten years ago. She had stepped in as a surrogate mother without hesitation, and Jack loved her for it.

He strolled into the kitchen and snagged a bite of the pineapple she was chopping. "Smells good in here."

She swatted at him with a towel. "My food always smells good. What have you been doing?"

"I went up to the volcano." He sat on a stool next to the counter. "It worries me, Anake." He'd called her aunt since he was a child.

"Ah, that thing has been talking for ages."

"I don't think we should discount the warnings this time. It is bringing in more foreigners."

She waved a wooden spoon at him. "Your papa was a foreigner once. Be nice. They bring in needed money. Off with you. I have work to do."

He snagged the plate of pineapple, winked, and headed out the back door. His home faced the ocean and all its glory. To the east grazed some cattle, to the west lay acres of sugar cane. It was a good life, if a lonely one. He popped a piece of the tart fruit into his mouth.

A breeze ruffled his hair. He closed his eyes and breathed deeply of the salt and seaweed. A shout from below caused him to open his eyes. An elderly man in a straw cone hat walked the shallow water and peered into a bottomless box in search for flounder. A woman, his wife maybe, picked up seaweed from the beach.

His life was peaceful, if only for … he glanced at the smoking volcano, and sighed. There was nothing he could do except watch it closely for signs of an eruption. If it did, they were all doomed.

As he continued to watch the waves and beachcombers, Miss Dillow, her dark hair hanging loose down her back, stopped to speak with the old woman. From that distance, she almost looked like a native, except for the more modern clothes and boots dangling from her hand.

He turned away, having no desire to get to know her, pretty as she was. When his fiancé had died, he'd sworn off women. Life on the island was hard. It took a certain type of woman to survive. If a native couldn't, then what made a petite thing like Lucy Dillow think she had what it took?

She laughed, the sound like music drifting to where he stood. He shook his head and marched to the barn. Time spent currying his horse might put his mind back where it belonged.

The ground rumbled under his feet. He stopped to see whether it would worsen. When it stopped altogether, he continued to the barn. Kilauea was only grumbling, but Jack intended to follow the geologists for a while the next day. Maybe he could find out whether there was cause for concern.

After grooming his horse, Jack headed back to the lanai and glanced toward the beach. Lucy sat on a patch of beach grass. Curiosity getting the better of him, he headed to join her.

She sat with a sketch pad on her lap. She paused in her drawing. "Good afternoon."

Her clipped tone alerted him to the fact that she wasn't feeling particularly friendly, at least not toward him. "What are you drawing?" Maybe kind words from him would soothe the hurt of his words earlier that afternoon.

"That flower. What's it called?"

He squatted next to the shrub with drooping pink blossoms and silvery heart-shaped leaves. "It's abutilon. You've captured it perfectly. You've a talent for drawing."

"There are so many exotic plants to entice me to wile away many hours." She closed her pad. "I spotted a sea turtle yesterday, poking its head above the waves to look around. It's like a slice of heaven here."

He held out a hand to help her to her feet. She frowned and accepted, sliding her hand from his almost immediately.

"My apologies for earlier," he said. "I'm only looking out for your welfare."

"I can look out for myself, thank you." She

turned the most amazing hazel eyes on him. Colors of green and gold flashed as her cheeks flushed. "I'm not a child and do not deserve to be treated as one."

"I said I was sorry."

She tilted her chin. "And so, I shall forgive you." She gathered up her shoes and shook the sand from them.

"Do you come here often? I haven't seen you on this beach before."

"I move around to keep my creative juices flowing." She straightened. "Is this a private beach?"

"No." He fell into step beside her as she headed up the hill.

He should let her go on her way without imposing his company, which it was clear she didn't want, on her. But, the lovely young woman intrigued him. Pretty, demure, with a love for her students, she showed fire under her calm exterior, and he found himself wanting to know her better.

A dangerous thing. While he might only be half native, he'd always thought he would stick to Hawaiian women … until this raven-haired beauty came into his life to challenge his resolutions.

The volcano rumbled. Lucy took a deep breath. "What do you make of it? I can't remember a morning when I didn't wake to my floor shaking."

"It's up to something." He put a hand on her elbow and guided her over a rough patch of ground. "I wish I knew whether it was a false alarm, like so many times before, or whether she'll blow."

"Will they evacuate?" She stopped and stared

at him, then back at the volcano. "I don't think I'd want to go. This could be the opportunity of a lifetime to see something so grand, so violent, yet so beautiful."

"You'd stay and put yourself in danger?"

"I'd keep a respectful distance." She shook the sand from her skirts. "Thank you for accompanying me, but I'm expected home for dinner." She held out her hand. "It was nice talking to you, Mr. Garrison."

"Please, call me Jack. We don't stand on formalities on the island."

"Then, I'm Lucy. Unless you're one of my students." She flashed a quick smile and headed down the road, arms swinging and her hair swaying with each step.

Jack watched until she was out of sight and headed to his own meal. He had no intentions of evacuating, either, if things came to that. He had a plantation to save. While he admired Lucy's spunk, her family didn't belong there. Everyone knew people from the mainland weren't as hearty as islanders. They'd perish for sure. He would need to convince her, somehow, to leave if the need arose.

"Who was the woman?" Anake handed him a plate.

He sat at the polished wood table. "The missionary's daughter, Lucy Dillow."

"Ah, she teaches the little ones English. Very pretty." She waggled her eyebrows.

"No matchmaking." He pointed his fork at her. "I gave up such notions a long time ago."

"But you are so young. Not even thirty. You

need a woman and children." She filled a plate for herself and joined him. "I worry for you."

"I'm fine." More than fine, actually. The plantation kept him plenty busy.

"This house is too big for the two of us."

Jack knew Anake was lonely after the death of her husband two years before, but he couldn't marry just to assuage the loneliness, hers or his. He would only marry for love, and to a woman who loved the island as much as he did. He bit into the savory pineapple covered pork, the tastes bursting on his tongue.

A fragrant breeze blew through the window. A bird sang from a tree outside. He had all he needed. Why borrow trouble?

When he'd finished, he took a mug of coffee to the lanai and sat in a curved wooden chair as was his nightly custom. He glanced again at Kilauea. The sky burned a deep orange above the crater.

The sleeping giant was definitely waking up.

2

Lucy woke to the usual shaking of her floor. She stretched and smiled, thinking on the handsome, dark Jack Garrison. She should have given the poor guy a chance to make amends a few days ago, but having him flounder at an apology had provided too much entertainment.

Before she could dress, her mother barged in the room. "Get dressed, quickly, and meet your father and I in the kitchen." Her mother tossed her a dress. "Come on, now. Don't dawdle."

The urgency in her voice spurred Lucy to action. Another shake had her grabbing a hold of her bureau. She stumbled to the window. The plume of smoke above Kilauea was the tallest she'd seen it in the year she'd lived on the island.

She dressed and rushed into the kitchen. One of the geologists, Mr. Woodward, she thought his name was, stood in the doorway. Lucy skidded to a halt.

"School is canceled for a while, dear," Lucy's father said. "The island is being evacuated."

Lucy sagged into a chair. "What has happened, Papa?"

He glanced at Mr. Woodward. "Sir, if you would be so kind as to explain."

Mr. Woodward nodded. "It's strictly a precaution, Miss. The magma in the crater is gone."

"Define gone." Lucy narrowed her eyes. "It was that way the other day."

"It has simply drained. Until we are able to figure out what has happened, and after much consideration, we think it best to evacuate. If you would be so kind as to help us spread the warning, we would appreciate it."

Lucy hadn't been able to get close enough to the crater for days. Was the draining what had caused the daily shaking of the earth? Now that it had drained … what did it all mean?

Papa nodded and stood. "Thank you, sir. But my family will not be leaving the island. Those we minister to will need us. We will draw back to a safe distance."

"Will it erupt?" Lucy planted her hands on the table top and pushed to her feet. "How long do we have?"

"We don't know." Mr. Woodward turned to go. "God go with you, Mr. Dillow and family."

"What do I need to do?" Lucy glanced from her mother to her father.

"We need to first find out where the islanders are going, those that choose to stay, anyway." Papa clapped his hat on his head. "If you could perhaps make the rounds of your students, that would help immensely. Your mother will pack our things."

Lucy nodded, her heart in her throat, and followed her father outside. She glanced one way, then the other. Which way? How soon before the danger took the option away from her? Which of her students needed her the most?

She watched in horror as the tower of smoke over the volcano continued to grow. Soon, the sun would be cloaked in gray and the once sunny island would be cast into dusk. She chose to go right and dashed to the end of the street. She'd start there and work her way back.

An hour later, only one family decided to evacuate to the island of Maui where they had family. The others planned to withdraw to the northern tip of the island.

Exhausted, Lucy sat outside a rustic café and pinned her hair off her neck. Running from door-to-door had left her covered in perspiration and burdened with how they would care for all those who wanted to stay if the volcano did erupt. Papa would say to trust God.

Lucy glanced at the volcano. She would do her best.

A loud boom sounded. Lucy leaped to her feet as a large boulder was thrust into the air. She screamed and covered her mouth. When no lava flowed from the volcano, she joined the throng that raced to witness the excitement. As she ran, the ash cloud covered the sun of a spring day in May, thrusting it into night. The temperature dropped several degrees.

"Lucy!" Her mother stood in the doorway of their home. "Come back."

"I have to see it, Mama." She increased her speed, stumbling when the road cracked under her, dropping two feet. She leaped over the opening and continued. If the danger increased, or a more violent explosion occurred, she would return home to help her mother to safety, but not before. Her sheltered life left little opportunity for excitement, and she didn't intend to miss out.

Army trucks sped past, skirting around the worst sections of road, on their way to the top of the mountain. Several of them yelled for the sightseers to go home, but none listened.

Jack galloped past on his horse, glancing over his shoulder at her as he did. She almost cried out for him to stop and give her a lift, but realized the futility of it all. He'd made his opinion on her curiosity clear. His hat blew off his head. She paused long enough to grab it and keep it from rolling down the mountain.

By the time she arrived, short of breath, and shivering from the chill of the day, a large crowd had gathered. Soldiers formed a line to try to keep the spectators at a safe distance.

Spying Jack, Lucy skirted around the barricade formed with soldiers and made her way to where Jack spoke with a geologist. Two other men stood around a large boulder off to one side.

"The poor fool didn't have a chance," the geologist said.

"I brought your hat." Lucy strained on tiptoes to see around them. "Was someone injured?"

"A man was killed, crushed by that boulder," Mr. Woodward said, approaching from behind them. "A journalist. These people should not be here." He glanced at Lucy.

"I can help." She squared her shoulders. "I'm a fair hand at drawing. I can watch a few hours each day and record any changes. I'm sure you don't have enough people to watch around the clock." She studied the area around her. "I can bring a stool and sit over there. I'll draw the area on the first day, then each time I come. You'll be able to tell if anything has been disturbed." How could he refuse her offer? If he said no, she'd come anyway. Nothing short of the military denying her the right would keep her away.

"She can draw very well," Jack admitted, replacing his hat on his head. "Perhaps, if she stays far enough back—"

"See?" Lucy practically bounced on her toes. "I can do this."

Mr. Woodward rubbed his chin. "I suppose if Mr. Garrison says it is all right. He knows these people better than we do."

"Thank you." Lucy grabbed Jack's hand. A spark ran up her arm and she pulled away, her face heating at her forwardness.

"I'll take my turn at watch, too," Jack said. "As soon as I have my cattle moved. I'll be finished and able to take a shift by tomorrow evening."

"Good." Mr. Woodward rubbed his hands together. "If we get a few more willing to help, we should have ample warning if this ancient girl decides to turn nasty."

"I'll start tonight." Excitement welled in Lucy.

Other than teaching, she had done so little to help others. This could be her chance to make her mark in the world. If Kilauea erupted, and she was able to provide ample warning, thus saving lives, she had fulfilled a great purpose for her life.

She grinned at Jack, nodded at Mr. Woodward, and headed home to battle with her mother. There was no way Mama would allow Lucy to do what she planned without a fight. Hopefully, Papa would side with his daughter.

As their only living child, Lucy's brother having died of smallpox as a young child, she had been sheltered, protected, and kept under her mother's thumb. At the age of nineteen, Lucy was a woman grown and wanted to be treated as such. Mama would have to let her do this.

She made her way home much slower than she had dashed away. She found her mother in the kitchen packing a box with food.

"You're back." Mama gave her a stern look. "What possessed you to run down the street like you have no manners?"

"I wanted to see what was going on." Lucy grabbed a mango from the box and tossed it up and down in her hand. "I've volunteered to watch the volcano a few hours each evening and draw what is happening."

"Absolutely not."

"This is something I can do to help the islanders, Mama." She set the fruit back in the box. "I don't like to disobey, but this is something I must do."

"I put my foot down."

On Lucy's wishes and desires, as usual. "I am sorry, but I *am* doing this."

"We'll see what your father says." She turned

her back and grabbed a pot from a cupboard, adding it to the box. "Pack your things. We're leaving as soon as your father returns."

"What was your desire for your life, Mama?" Lucy leaned against the counter. "Did you ever feel as if you were meant to do something grand?"

"I've wanted nothing more than to be a wife and mother. God granted me that wish. I've no reason to try for dreams in the clouds."

"Well, I want to be something more than that. I want to leave a legacy. I can do that by drawing the changes that are happening and saving them for future generations." She closed her eyes, imagining a book made with her drawings.

"You shape young minds. That is enough."

"Not for me." She wrapped her arms around her mother and rested her cheek against her back. "Don't be angry. Have a happy heart for me."

"It's too dangerous," Mama whispered. "You're my only child."

"I'm an adult. I love you." She turned her and cupped her mother's face. "I'll be fine. Hawaii would never hurt me."

"Said a foolish man right before a giant wave sinks his boat." Mama smiled and patted her cheek. "I'll say no more about this, but I will pray, very hard, every minute you're on that cursed mountain."

"Agreed."

"I've always wanted to design clothing." She stepped back and resumed her work. "Maybe it's time I picked up my lead pencil again."

"You can borrow mine." Lucy headed to her room to pack.

Instead of fighting, as was their usual way of disagreeing, they had conversed as adults. Maybe she had been treated as a child for so long because she had acted like one. Tears and pouting always worked with Papa, but drove a wedge between her and her mother. Today was the first day toward a new relationship between mother and daughter.

She tossed her clothes into a battered suitcase, and her art supplies into a small tote, and dragged them onto the veranda, or lanai, as it was called in Pahala. Where would they stay if they left their home? Surely, Papa didn't intend for them to live in communal housing?

"The car is here," Papa called from the street. "Hurry. The road is getting congested."

"We're ready." Mama lugged a heavy box outside, which Papa promptly took, then headed in for another one.

After stowing her things in the back seat, Lucy went back inside for their bedding. She would look on all that was happening as a grand adventure, despite the discomforts that loomed ahead of them. Papa and Mama would minister to the islanders, and Lucy would continue the children's lessons until the time for her to watch the volcano. Things would return to normal in a few days, with little harm done.

~

With the help of a couple of paniolos, Jack rounded up the cattle and herded them into the corral. Tomorrow morning, they would drive them north. The hired hands could watch the cattle as Jack watched Kilauea and made sure that Lucy's impulsive offer of help didn't get her into trouble.

He rode into town and stopped where Lucy and her family loaded the back of a battered car. "Where is everyone headed?"

"North to the Kohala Coast. They are setting up a refugee camp there." Mr. Dillow straightened from placing a box into the trunk. "I am Henry Dillow." He offered his hand.

Jack bent down to shake it. "I'm Jack Garrison. I've met your daughter."

"At the crater, I presume." He cast an indulgent glance at Lucy. "She is smitten with the thing."

"Many of us are." He winked at Lucy. "I'm sure I'll see you at the camp. The army is making me leave the plantation."

Lucy ducked her head as her mother glowered between her daughter and Jack. He didn't mind. He had grown up with prejudice because of his mixed blood his entire life. His day wouldn't be ruined because a malihini looked down her nose at him.

He tipped his hat at Lucy and continued to see where his help might be appreciated somewhere else. All through the village, people were loading wagons, hand carts, and carrying packs on their backs. He stopped and pulled a young girl, no more than four, onto the front of his saddle and her older brother on the back. "I'll carry them," he told the frazzled mother. He knew the family. The husband spent most of his time drinking away the meager salary he earned fishing.

He rode slowly so the mother could keep up, and headed to the coast. Three hours later, which he suspected might be early evening, it was hard to tell with the sky dark, they arrived where refugees were being crowded into an abandoned community building. He shuddered to think of so many people under one roof.

Spotting the Dillows, he turned the children back over to their mother and climbed off his horse. Reins in hand, he approached Lucy. "See that small building over there?" He pointed to a house that was little more than a shack. "It belongs to me. Your family is welcome to stay there."

She smiled and whispered something to her father. He nodded at Jack and carried a box inside their temporary home.

Now, Jack needed to find the owner and purchase the property. He had no idea why he had made the gesture, especially with the way Mrs. Dillow sent cold glances his way, but the thought of Lucy crowded in with hundreds of others made his blood chill.

Lucy would need a way to get to the crater. If she walked, she'd spend most of her day traveling back and forth. He patted the neck of his horse. "Guess the old mare back at the plantation will work well enough, right boy?" He would deliver the horse in the morning, and hoped Lucy knew how to ride.

He had just turned to go when Lucy ran up to him. "Thank you so much. I was hoping to find a place to hold a couple of hours of school each day. I can hold it out here, in front of this cottage."

"You're welcome, but it isn't much." His neck flushed.

"It's more than a lot of people have. My family

is grateful."

"Even your mother?" He tried to bite off the words, but failed.

Lucy sighed. "Don't pay her any mind, please. She will work things out in her own time."

"How do you plan on getting back and forth to the crater?"

"I have a bicycle that Papa will fetch for me."

He shook his head, swinging into the saddle. "You won't get far on the destroyed roads on a bike. Can you ride a horse?"

She nodded.

"I have a gentle one at home. I'll bring her tomorrow. Good day, Lucy."

She stepped back, allowing him to swing the horse's head around. Once she could no longer see his face, he laughed. She planned on riding a bicycle in the frilly dresses she wore? He would have liked to have seen that.

Perhaps, Lucy needed to dress more like a native. His horse flicked his ears at Jack's laugh. Or perhaps, she could forgo the more modern style for a loose fitting cotton skirt and blouse. Anything except the straight hemmed style she wore. Of course, a horse wouldn't be much better. Maybe he should bring her one of Anake's muumuus.

Another hour of searching and he found the owner of the shack he sent the Dillows to, and was able to purchase another one for himself and Anake. The greedy foreigner was going to make a lot of money off the misfortune of others.

By the time he returned to the plantation, Anake had packed enough food to last months, and folded clothing into boxes. How in the world were they supposed to transport it all? He sure hoped his horse didn't mind pulling a cart.

Night was falling by the time they headed for the coast. His housekeeper, not wanting to wait until morning, insisted on riding the mare Jack was going to lend to Lucy. The old woman rode astride, her voluminous dress covering her legs and most of the horse.

"I still say we could have waited until morning," he said.

"Smell that?" She wrinkled her flat nose. "The air is foul. I refuse to breathe it for one moment more. I need the fresh ocean air."

"If the wind shifts, the coast won't smell fresh either." His stomach rumbled.

She dug in the pack hanging on her shoulders and tossed him sweet rice wrapped in seaweed. "This will do for now. The men will bring the cattle and feed in the morning. No worries."

Jack glanced over his shoulder at the plantation. Would he see it again, or would the angry god in the volcano take the only thing Jack had left?

3

Lucy stood on a small hill on the western coast of Hawaii and closed her eyes. So far, the wind hadn't shifted and the ash cloud stayed over the village of Pahala. Because of the fresh air and gentle ocean breeze, she had elected to hold school on the beach that morning, and waited for her students to arrive.

Gratitude for Jack's generous offer of a place of their own, however small, filled her. She'd slept well on the small sofa, considering the looming threat of Kilauea, and stood ready to face the day.

She opened her eyes at a far off and barely heard rumble, as more smoke billowed from the mountain. She sighed, wishing the mountain would either quiet down or do whatever it was going to do so life could get back to normal. They'd been at refuge for a week and, other than small, scattered rocks, her drawings showed nothing compared to the giant boulder that had killed the poor journalist. Still, she valued the solitary time spent at the crater.

"Good morning, Lucy."

She shaded her eyes. Jack stood on the beach, his features in shadow, the sun at his back and highlighting his dark hair with a deep indigo. She rarely saw the handsome rancher, as she stayed busy with her students, the crater, and helping her mother distribute needed food to the refugees. "Good morning, Jack."

He climbed the small hill to stand beside her. "You're out mighty early this morning."

"I come here to think, before the students arrive. You must be going stir crazy without your plantation."

He nodded. "I spend a lot of time riding back and forth checking on things. My housekeeper, Anake, is happy here, though. That's important to me."

"Your aunt?"

"No. I've just always called her that. She's been with my family for a very long time." He stared out to sea. "The waves are choppy this morning, but the water is warm. Would you like to take a stroll along the water's edge?"

She noticed his bare feet and wet, rolled up pants. "It looks as if you've already been wading."

"I love the feel of wet sand between my toes." He grinned, sending her heart into somersaults. He held out his hand. "Come on. You've time."

She slipped off her shoes and grasped his hand. "My mother will kill me if she finds out."

He stiffened. "Because you're with me?"

"No, because it isn't ladylike behavior."

She released his hand and dashed to the water. Her mother would be upset that she was behaving so carelessly with Jack, but as a foreigner to the island, she had few friends. She wasn't about to push anyone away, especially one who looked as good as he did. She cut a sideways glance to where he stood a few feet away.

Jack was right. The water was heavenly. She hiked her dress to her knees and let the waves kiss her ankles and seaweed strands tickle her legs. Mama would definitely have a conniption fit if she were to see Lucy now. She dropped her hem, no longer caring if it got wet, and opened her arms wide to embrace the sun.

"You look as if you belong here," Jack said.

"I never want to leave. This place felt like home the moment I set foot on its shore."

The sounds of laughing children pulled her from the water. "Play time is over, I'm afraid. Thank you."

"I'm here every morning. Will I see you tomorrow?"

The earnest look in his eyes dried her mouth. Was it possible he enjoyed her company as much as she enjoyed his?

"Yes," she whispered. Nothing would keep her away, short of the island sinking into the sea.

Sliding her feet back into the simple shoes she chose to wear instead of more complicated, fashionable footwear, she tossed him a grin and hurried to greet her students. Her face flushed with their good-natured teasing about her playing in the waves with Jack. She'd been caught, and there was no way her mother wouldn't find out. She didn't care. She could make her own decisions about her friends. If Mama would make more of an effort, she wouldn't be plagued with loneliness. The natives were friendly and would welcome her with open arms.

She placed blankets on the grass and situated her students by age. "We'll work on arithmetic before heading into our language lesson. Does anyone have any questions about yesterday's assignment?"

A little girl, Anna, ten-years-old, raised her hand. "Kumu, are we going to die?"

Lucy gasped. "Why would you ask such a thing?"

"My Makua k<u>a</u>ne says the gods are angry at all the white people on the island and will cause the sky to catch fire."

Heavens. Lucy clutched the lace at her throat. If her father thought such a thing, it was a wonder the child was allowed to attend school.

"No, little one." Jack leaned against a palm tree. "The gods are not angry. The volcano has spoken to us since the beginning of time. Why should she stop speaking now?"

"What is she saying?"

He grinned. "That we should be kind to the visitors." He winked in Lucy's direction, then sauntered off, his long-legged gait taking him out of sight within seconds.

"Well." Lucy clapped her hands. "That was well said. Back to our lessons, students."

"What do you see at the volcano?" Another student asked.

Lucy sighed. There would be no lessons until their curiosity was sated. "A lot of smoke and ash."

"No lava?"

"No lava." Lucy smiled. "She's letting off steam is all. We're far enough away as to be safe if she gets really angry. Does no one want to learn today?"

They shook their heads.

"We want to collect seaweed and fish to help feed our families," Anna said.

How could Lucy say no? With all the help her family was giving others, they could very well be hungry soon themselves. "Very well. Off you go. But, I expect your full attention tomorrow."

She folded up the blankets and carried them to her temporary home. After depositing them in a corner of the front room, she changed her clothes to her riding habit.

"What were you thinking?" Mama stood in the doorway of the one bedroom. "Frolicking in the ocean with that man?"

"We were only enjoying the morning." Lucy grabbed a wide-brimmed straw hat. Her pale skin burned easily. If she weren't careful, she'd be as dark as the islanders, and Mama would have something else to carry on about.

"It wasn't proper."

"It's 1924, Mama." Lucy took a deep breath to keep her temper under control.

"Mr. Garrison is not the type of man your father and I hope you will marry. Maybe it is time to send you to a girl school on the mainland."

Lucy jerked around. "You wouldn't!"

"We will consider it if it will keep you from making a grave mistake." Mama put her fists on her slim hips. "We want the best for you, dear."

"We're only friends. I don't have many."

"We aren't here to make friends."

"I am." Tears burned Lucy's eyes. "I'm never leaving here."

"When your father mentioned coming here, I knew it wasn't a good idea to bring you. I should have listened to my instincts." She turned and left, calling over her shoulder for Lucy to be careful on that cursed horse and on the volcano.

She hadn't wanted Lucy to come? Must Mama always force her own unhappiness on her daughter?

Lucy brushed away the streaming tears and dashed out the door. She kept running until she reached the paddock where Jack kept the horses. As he had done every day, the gentle animal was saddled and waiting.

"At least she can't say we can't be friends." She buried her face in the horse's neck. "You're only an animal."

"Are you okay?" Jack stepped from around his horse.

"I didn't see you there." She ducked her head to hide her tears. "My mother and I had a disagreement. One of many."

"She found out about this morning, didn't she?" He slipped the bridle onto his horse. "I'm sorry."

"It isn't you." Lucy looked up. "She wants to send me to the mainland to some girl school in order to find me a suitable husband. She lives in the dark ages."

"You wouldn't find it hard to settle here, being from the mainland?" His earnest gaze made her uncomfortable, as if he could see into the deepest parts of her and somehow find her lacking.

"Why should I? If I stay here, even when my father feels led to move on to his next ministry field, I'll become one of your people, over time. Garrison isn't a native name. Your father carved out a place for himself."

"By marrying a well-loved native." He grabbed the reins to both horses and led them from the paddock.

Lucy jogged after them. "Then, I'll marry a native."

~

Jack's heart almost stopped. She was naïve. He shouldn't encourage her by spending time with her, but he knew the loneliness she must feel. Until her arrival, he had embraced his life alone. She showed him he wanted a wife, after all, but it couldn't be her. It was a mistake to become her friend.

"Perhaps you should listen to your parents." It pained him to say so, but staying on the island, expecting to be welcomed with open arms, was looking at things through clouded eyes. Very few of the native men would be willing to toss aside tradition to marry a haole.

"Perhaps you should mind your own business." She put one foot into the stirrup and swung into the saddle. "Please step aside. I have work to do."

"Please." He grabbed the bridle to her horse. "I don't mean to hurt you. It's only that you need to understand the difficulties of what you're asking."

"Don't worry yourself. I have tough skin. Nothing you can say will hurt me." She yanked the reins free and rode away.

What a brave, proud, foolish girl. She was headed for heartbreak, and there was nothing Jack could do about it.

It was his shift at the volcano, but he'd bet his hat that was where Lucy was headed. He groaned and swung into the saddle. Maybe she shouldn't be left alone in her state. A blind man could tell she'd been crying. If he hurried, he could catch up with her.

He found her stopped on the road by three military men. By Lucy's body language—

hands on hips, head thrown back—she was giving the young men a piece of her mind.

He dismounted and approached the group. "What's going on?"

"We're trying to tell this little lady that the volcano is dangerous and no one but authorized personnel is allowed at the crater," one of men said.

"And I'm telling them that I am authorized." Lucy huffed and shook her head. "They refuse to listen to reason."

"We are both assigned shifts to watch the volcano for signs of danger," Jack said. "If you check with the geologists, you will see the names Lucy Dillow and Jack Garrison."

The cocky young man pulled a clipboard from under the seat of the jeep. "Oh, here they are. Sorry about the confusion." He grinned at his comrades.

Lucy stormed past them, leading the mare. Jack followed. "Hold up. They were only having a bit of fun."

"At my expense." She whirled on him like a

typhoon.

"They're bored with nothing else to do but question those wanting to watch the volcano."

As far as he knew, there were no restrictions to anyone wanting to visit the crater. Not yet, at least. He glanced to the top of Kilauea. Already a crowd gathered, consisting mostly of tourists in fancy dresses and big hats. The soldiers had seen a pretty girl and wanted to pass a bit of time. He doubted they meant her any harm.

Lucy stuck her pretty little nose in the air and continued her march. Jack didn't blame the soldiers. As much as he told himself he shouldn't spend time with the school teacher, he found himself drawn to her like a moth to a flame. It was quite possible it wouldn't be her left with a broken heart, but himself left scorched when she left with her parents.

When they reached the top, Lucy pulled her sketchbook from underneath a rock and perched on the rock, pencil in hand. Jack sat on another boulder and watched the tourists act as if the smoking crater was cause for celebration.

The air smelled of smoke and sulphur. Ash fell like a gentle rain, coating Lucy's hair with flecks of gray. She didn't seem to notice as she drew, occasionally swiping her hand across her pad. He wanted to glance at her drawing, but since she had yet to speak a word, he decided she wanted to be left alone.

He hunched over, his hands dangling between his knees, and watched as Mr. Woodward, and a man Jack had yet to meet, walked the perimeter of the crater, taking notes on a clipboard. He pushed to his feet and met them halfway around. "Gentlemen. Is there anything new to report?"

"Thanks to that little lady over there, we have a good record of a large number of rocks being cast from the crater each day." They glanced at Lucy. "Usually, she is sitting much closer. Today, she seems focused on the tourists."

"It isn't time for her shift," Jack said. He shuddered at the thought of Lucy sitting close enough to possibly be struck by one of the rocks she sketched. "The air seems more foul today."

Mr. Woodward nodded. "I'm afraid she's going to blow soon. These tourists have no business here. One man has lost his life, we don't need any more fatalities."

"I can help keep them away." Jack would like nothing better. A simmering cauldron wasn't to be messed with. "It's too late to do anything about today, but tomorrow, along with the military's help, we can post notices and run off the sightseers."

"Good idea. I put you in charge." Mr. Woodward clapped him on the shoulder. "Make sure that Lucy stays well back from the edge. We'd hate to lose her."

"I will, sir." Gladly.

Jack moved back to Lucy's side and glanced at her drawing. She had sketched a realistic rendering of the group of tourists standing in front of the plume of smoke. She glanced up, then closed her pad.

"I need to move closer," she said. "I can't see the changes from back here. Walk with me?"

He nodded and told her of his conversation

with Mr. Woodward, including the man's wish that Lucy stay well back. He waited for the explosion he knew was coming.

"I can't do my job effectively if everyone insists on treating me like a fragile hibiscus flower!" She stomped her foot. "I'm as capable as any man of noting the danger. I thought you, of all people, would side with me. Aren't we friends, Jack?"

A shadow passed over her eyes that had nothing to do with the smoke. "What if the volcano erupts while you're out here?"

"I'll run. Same as anyone else." She tucked her pad under her arm and moved closer to the crater.

The ground trembled. Jack grabbed Lucy's arm to keep her from falling. "This is what causes us concern."

"Stop it. The ground has been doing this for weeks." She pulled free and continued on her way.

The smoke cloud increased, causing the tourists to step back. "It's too dangerous, Lucy. Not just for you, but for me."

"If you're concerned, bring the horses closer." She perched on another rock and prepared to sketch again.

He tugged his hat more firmly on his head and stormed to the horses. Foolish girl! Couldn't she read the signs? She was going to get herself killed.

He untied the horses from the straggly bush that held them and hurried to go back to her side. Before he got there, the earth gave a groan and a mighty shudder. Rocks exploded from the crater in a mushroom cloud.

Lucy turned to him, her eyes wide.

Without pause, Jack released the mare with a slap to her rump and swung onto his horse's saddle. He galloped toward Lucy as she sprinted his way. Another explosion, larger than the first, rained stones around them. One bounced off Lucy's shoulder, almost bringing her to her knees. The tourists screamed and scattered.

"Take my hand!" Jack stretched out his arm. Lucy grasped hold and he swung her up behind him.

With a mighty roar, Kilauea expressed her anger. The sky darkened. Ash fell, and the smoke cloud cast day into night.

With his heart in his throat, and Lucy's arms tight around his waist, Jack raced down the mountain as fast as the horse could go without breaking a leg.

The earth's fury had been unleashed.

4

Lucy groaned and slumped against Jack's back. Her shoulder ached something fierce. She glanced over her shoulder as the crowd dashed down the mountain, rocks and ash falling like gray snow around them, making them all look the same, so thick was the volcanic ash on their skin. Fiery rocks filled the air like rockets shooting into the sky. Screams and the sound of falling rocks resounded. Lucy closed her eyes and held tight to Jack's waist.

The scene at the refugee camp wasn't much different. The refugees scattered like chickens, dashing in all directions. "Stop them, Jack! They're safer here."

"Not until I have your shoulder tended to." He slid from his horse and pulled Lucy into his arms, jarring her shoulder. "You're my first priority."

She cried out against the pain and buried her face in his neck. She wouldn't cry. Not now. She needed to be strong. "Mama will help." Along with a gigantic lecture on why she hadn't wanted Lucy to go to the volcano in the first place.

Jack carried her through the open door of her

family's hut. "It doesn't look as if anyone is here."

A pan of fish sat on the stove, the gas turned off. A half-peeled apple rested on the counter. Her mother must have fled like so many others. "Where will everyone go? This is the farthest tip of the island."

Her shoulder throbbed, stealing her breath. For the first time in a long time, she felt like a small child who wanted the ministrations of their mama's hands. Tears pricked her eyelids.

"I'll take you to Anake. She won't have run." Jack jogged down the street to a hut not much different than the one Lucy was living in.

"Anake!"

"There you are." A woman as round as she was short stepped through an open door and wiped her hands on a red apron. "What has happened?"

"The volcano is blowing. Lucy has been injured." Jack gently laid her on a faded sofa. "Her parents are gone." He rattled off comments like the volcano spewed out rocks.

"Wait here."

Jack knelt beside the sofa and smoothed Lucy's hair away from her face. "I knew I shouldn't have allowed you to go up there."

"It was my decision." She laid back, relishing in the feel of his touch. Her feelings might be inappropriate in so many ways, but with her shoulder paining her, she threw propriety to the wind. "How long do we have until she really blows?"

"I don't know. Anake, hurry!"

"I'm here." She pushed him out of the way and

leaned over Lucy, her brown, round face creased with worry. "Go keep watch, Jack. You can't be here."

He met Lucy's gaze and nodded. "I'll be right outside."

"This will hurt. I am sorry." Anake peeled Lucy's shirt off, tossing the ruined fabric to the floor. "I'm afraid it's melted a bit to your skin."

Lucy hissed and bit her lip. "I understand."

"You have a bad burn." She dipped her fingers into a jar and spread a jelly like substance on Lucy's shoulder. The burning eased. "You will be sore for many days." She wound a clean white cloth around the wound, then pulled a voluminous blouse over Lucy's head. She giggled like one of Lucy's students. "You are drowning."

Lucy grabbed her hand. "I am very grateful." The loose fitting garment flowed around her, not increasing the discomfort of her shoulder.

"You rest." She patted her hand and slipped free. "I have tea brewing. It will help you sleep."

"No, we have to leave." She struggled to sit up.

"The volcano cannot hurt us here. Rest." She pushed Lucy back to a prone position. "Not everyone has run away in panic."

Perhaps she was right. Maybe her parents only left because someone needed them. Surely, knowing that Lucy was on the volcano, they would not have left her unless someone else was in dire need.

"May I come in now?" Jack called from the front porch.

"Yes."

Jack rushed to her side and cupped her cheek.

"How are you feeling?"

"Burned and bruised." She forced a smile, trying to relieve the worry lines on his face. "Thank you for getting me out of there. Was anyone else injured?"

He hung his head. "They carried a woman's body down. I don't know whether she made it. Others were injured, same as you."

"Is the mountain finished?"

"I don't think so. I think she's just warming up. There's a terrific lightening show if you're up to sitting on the lanai."

"Yes, please." From there, she could witness the spectacular works from the safety of Jack's porch.

He scooped her back into his arms and settled her into a rocking chair. "Are you sure you're okay?"

"I'm fine."

Lightning flashed through a dark sky. Occasionally, a rock, crimson with fire, added to the display. "It's glorious."

Jack chuckled. "You're a strange woman, Lucy Dillow. Most women would want nothing more to do with a mountain that almost killed them."

A heavy rain began to fall, heavy with ash. Within minutes, the dirt road outside the hut was nothing more than a mud pit. Jack's mare plodded toward them.

"I've got to take care of the horses."

"I'll be fine." Lucy patted his arm. "Anake is here." Really, he didn't need to hover. She was content to watch the show in the distance while he did the work that needed doing. With her wound cleaned and dressed, she felt ten times better, although her heart rate did increase at his concern.

She did her best to squelch her feelings. Jack was doing nothing more than what any gentleman would do when a woman was injured. She mustn't read more into his actions than what was needed. Still, it didn't hurt a girl to dream, just a little. She fell asleep to the most spectacular sky show she'd ever seen, not waking until Jack gently shook her.

"You're chilled. Let's get you inside."

"I'm no more cold than you. You're dripping." She straightened, irritating her shoulder.

Water, the color of gray ash, dripped from his hair and clothes. She used a corner of her blouse to wipe it from his face. "Get inside. I can walk."

He started to put his arm around her waist, then stopped. "You're right. I'll only get you wet." He watched as she made her way inside and to the sofa before disappearing into a back room, returning minutes later in dry clothes, his hair slicked back from his face. He truly was a handsome man, and showed her each time she saw him that the inside was just as beautiful as the out.

She sighed and settled back on the sofa, the nap having done her a wonder of good. The sound of banging pots came from the kitchen area. She wanted to offer help, but knew the futility of it. She would let them treat her as an invalid until morning, but no more. She intended to earn her keep and desperately needed to find her parents.

"Do you need anything?"

"I'm worried about my parents."

"I'll go look for them."

She shook her head. "Wait until the rain stops. You won't be any good to any of us if you catch a chill." She bit her bottom lip and stared out the window. Surely, the rain would stop soon. Then, what? Would their fiery friend spit more rock and ash into the air, or would she really blow, sending rivers of lava to run into the sea? "I dropped my sketch pad when you swung me onto your horse.

All her hard work gone, buried beneath rock and volcanic dust.

~

Jack knew the moment the words left Lucy's lips that he would be heading back up the mountain to fetch her drawings. After a quick dinner, he saddled his poor horse again, hoping that his decision to put a smile on Lucy's face wouldn't result in disaster.

Kilauea continued to growl as the horse picked its way over stones and around boulders. A few fools, such as he, moved closer to the crater to get a better look. He halted long enough to grab Lucy's pad from the ground and tuck it into his shirt, then left the horse tethered to a scorched bush before moving to the edge.

In the distance, people thronged the military base. Vehicles lined up for the purpose of evacuation. Over it all hung clouds pregnant with ash. Lightning still struck over the top of the volcano. The air crackled with electricity, causing his hair to stand on end. He carefully made his way around a rock that had to have weighed several tons.

The mouth of the crater had widened. He

pulled a handkerchief from his pocket and held it over his nose against the thick dust coating the air. Instinct told him that the volcano wasn't finished. Still, the awesome sight before him held him spellbound. Lucy would be in awe at the sight.

He turned toward the hotel and tourist destination Volcano House. Several people were loading suitcases into vehicles in an attempt to flee, while still others came in a group to see the volcano. If Jack had his way, no civilian would be allowed on the mountain until the military gave the all clear. In fact, he chose to heed his advice and marched back to his horse. Staying only put himself in further danger.

Lucy's pad dug into his rib cage. Her injury was a blessing in disguise, whether she realized it or not, and would keep her safe in the village.

Back on his horse, he headed for the military base in search of Mr. and Mrs. Dillow. Although Lucy didn't complain, he could tell worry over her parents clouded her mind.

"Mr. Dillow!" Jack waved his hat at Lucy's parents who helped an elderly woman into a jeep.

"Have you seen my Lucy?" Mrs. Dillow bustled toward him. "We were asked to help these people. My nerves are stretched thin."

"Lucy is safe and waiting for you."

Mr. Dillow reached up a hand. "Thank you for coming to let us know."

Jack glanced over his shoulder at the volcano. "These people need to leave quickly. She isn't finished blowing."

Mr. Dillow nodded. "We'll be along shortly.

Give Lucy our love."

"Yes, sir." Jack reined the horse to the right, leaving the Dillows behind. He wasn't much of a praying man, but cast one for their safety toward heaven.

What caused a husband and wife to put their lives in jeopardy for strangers? Jack always thought of himself as a good man, but family would always come first for him. If his parents were still alive, would he have been able to set aside his responsibility to them and help those, foreigners in particular, who had no business being so close to the danger in the first place? He didn't know.

He rode his horse to the small shack he used as a temporary barn. After removing the saddle, he brushed the ash from the animal's coat, while still pondering what his role might be in the disaster unfolding. He glanced out the door to where Lucy stood on the porch, a hot breeze ruffling her hair and loose-fitting clothes. From that distance, she looked like an island maiden waiting for her love to return. Could he get past the fact that she wasn't an islander and let his heart go where it wanted? Could he handle the ridicule of the people he had grown up with and fall in love with her?

Did she watch for him, or was she worrying about not knowing where her parents were? He set the currying brush on a shelf and went to relieve her mind.

Her smile lit up the overcast day, confirming the fact that she did wait for him. He pulled her sketch pad from inside his shirt. "I found it."

She clasped it to her chest. "Thank you. This is

my legacy."

"Legacy?"

She plopped onto the rocker, leaving Jack to lean against the shaky porch railing. "I want to be something more than a missionary's daughter, teaching natives a language they don't really care to learn. Being here, in the middle of all this," she waved a hand at the volcano, "and being a fair hand at drawing … well, this I can leave for those who come after.

"God has a purpose for every one of his children. I like to think this is mine."

"What if your purpose is to only teach the keiki? Isn't that important enough?"

"If so, then God will have to remove the desire from my heart to do something more."

"I found your parents at the military base." He studied her face, not sure what he was looking for. "They seem content with their calling. They are helping people prepare to flee, those who chose not to come to this end of the island."

She nodded. "Their purpose is to minister to the heathens."

He wasn't sure how he felt about his people being called heathens, but let the comment slide. "They'll be by when they are finished."

"Thank you for searching, and for finding my drawings. You put yourself in possible danger for something you must think frivolous."

He almost told her he would do anything for her, but turned to stare at the ocean instead. Expressing his growing feelings for her, and raising her hopes of marrying a native in order to be accepted by those on the island, would do no one any good. He gave her parents another year at the most before they moved on, taking Lucy with them.

He'd also seen enough of their kind to know they wouldn't approve of her and him. The waves slapped the beach as thunder rolled over the mountain behind them, echoing the turmoil inside him. He should have left Lucy to her own and never gotten close. Minding his own business when she expressed a desire to help keep watch over Kilauea would have prevented the coming heartache. Just as the volcano was going to blow more fierce than before, his heart was going to lie in shattered pieces like the rocks strewn over the mountain.

"Have I said something to upset you?" Lucy stepped to his side. "If so, I apologize."

"No, you could never upset me." A lie to soothe her worry and increase his pain.

He stared into her beautiful face and cupped her cheek. He stared into eyes the color of seaweed and bit back the words of adoration that rested on his tongue.

She licked her lips, drawing his attention to their rosiness. He lowered his head, ready to taste of their sweetness.

"Lucy Dillow!" Mrs. Dillow's screeching words pierced through the love-laced fog in his head.

5

Lucy almost took a step behind Jack to escape her mother's wrath. Instead, she moved forward in an attempt to shield him.

"I was so worried, Mama." She forced a shaky grin and focused on her father, who frowned. Not the norm for his usual jovial self.

"It looks like it." Mama crossed her arms. "What are you wearing?"

"My housekeeper had to cut off her blouse," Jack said. "We had nothing else suitable."

"Heavens!" Mama clutched at the lace collar of her blouse. "You look like a native, no offense, Mr. Garrison. I'm much obliged that you cared for my daughter."

"None taken."

"He saved my life." Lucy lifted her chin and squared her shoulders. "If he hadn't have taken me on the back of his horse—"

"Enough!" Mama raised a hand. "I don't need to know the lurid details. "Come. It's time you came home. I can only pray your reputation hasn't been shattered."

Papa stepped forward and offered his hand to

Jack. "I trust you were respectable."

"Yes sir."

"Gracious, Mama!" Lucy stomped down the steps. "What do you take me for?" She turned and gazed on Jack, at the shadow of pain in his eyes, the rigidness of his shoulders. "Thank you."

He gave a curt nod and escaped to the sanctuary of his hut.

Lucy was marched to their small home like a wayward child and ordered to change. She needed help with her shoulder bandaged as it was, but she would rather eat ash than ask. She would somehow manage. How dare her parents treat her like a child? Couldn't they see how much help she was with the volcano?

Oh, no. She'd left her drawings with Jack. She plopped on the narrow bed that her parents shared. A slow smile spread across her face. She had a reason to see him again, with or without her parent's blessing.

The floor shuddered under her feet. She dashed to the one small window at the back of the cottage. The ash cloud in the distance had increased. The mountain's fury was building. How could she get closer to witness the event? Not so close as to be struck again, but near enough to witness the display?

With the thick clouds present over the island, and the day cast into a semi-darkness, the red glow over the mouth of Kilauea provided a bright contrast to the dreary day. Dread rose in Lucy's throat, threatening to choke her. No, she would trust Jack's judgment that they were safe on that end of the island. Even a lava flow would take a while to reach them, giving them plenty of warning in order to flee.

A knock sounded on the bedroom door. She turned. "Come in."

"Not changed yet, I see," her father said, joining her at the window. "I can guess you had quite the experience today."

"It was amazing." She grinned. "Other than a burn and some bruising, I'm fine."

He glanced toward the smoking giant. "I've heard a couple of others were not so lucky. Some people are missing."

"It isn't over yet, Papa."

"We'll be fine. God is watching over us." He sat on the bed. "Tell me of your stay with Mr. Garrison so I can ease your mother's mind."

"He's a complete gentleman. His housekeeper nursed my wounds and gave me a clean blouse." She took his hands. "You can trust me to do what is right, Papa."

"I know." He returned her smile. "But I am relieved to know that you had a chaperone."

"Not that mother will count a native as a sufficient one."

"Give her time, dear. She'll come to love these people as we do." He stood and gave her a gentle hug. "I'll send her in to help you change."

Seconds later, Mama must have been right outside the door, she entered. "I'm sorry. I should have realized you would need help."

"I would have managed."

"Rather than ask me for the help, I imagine."

Lucy stood still while her mother unbuttoned the row of shell buttons down the front of the blouse. "Jack is a good man, Mama. He saved me and found you."

"That may be the case, but he is not one of our kind."

She yanked back. "We are all God's children. How can you be so unkind? Aren't we here to minister to these people? Once they become Christians, we are all brothers and sisters in Christ."

Mama pursed her lips together. "Spiritually, yes."

Lucy sagged. "Oh, Mama, I feel so sorry for you. You are missing out on so much with that mindset."

"I fear the volcano and your infatuation with this island is dangerous for you. I've spoken with your father. We will be leaving after Christmas."

Seven months. "I will not leave. This is where I want to call home. I'm tired of traveling. Your calling is not my calling. I will be content to stay among these wonderful people and call them my family."

Mama grabbed a fresh blouse from a hook on the wall. "This discussion is over. I'm ready to live as a privileged person again."

The entire conversation was a waste. Mama would never see the beauty of the Hawaiian people, just as she couldn't see the same with American natives when they had spent time on a reservation. Seven months might not be a long while, but it would have to be enough for Lucy to convince her parents she meant to stay.

The floor trembled again. Mama groaned. "I can't stand this insufferable movement." She stormed from the room, leaving Lucy to button her blouse with one hand, as tears ran down her cheeks. She prayed for a softening of her mother's heart, and that she would learn to see others through God's eyes.

When she'd finished, she went to the kitchen to help her mother prepare a simple meal of rice, ham, and pineapple slices. The grumbling of the volcano provided a backdrop of eerie music as ash continued to fall and sour the air.

Was Jack watching the show from his window? Was he growing concerned, or did he still believe they were safe in their huts by the sea? Surely, if they weren't, he would come for her.

"Stop daydreaming and set the table." Mama thrust three plates at her.

The paleness of her skin and the tautness around her mother's mouth alerted Lucy to the real reason for her mother's sharp tongue. She was frightened and doing her best to rein in her terror. In the past, their missionary trips had been to safe places on the mainland. Now, they were thrust into a danger none of them were prepared to face.

Lucy set the plates on the counter and wrapped her good arm around her mother. "We'll be fine, Mama. I promise."

Mama sniffed. "That ... thing out there, is ready to kill us."

"Not here. All we'll experience is some darkness, muddy rain, and falling ash. Unpleasant, but not deadly. Come." She led her to the table.

"You sit, and I'll finish dinner. Papa, fetch Mama a cup of tea, please."

"That sounds like the perfect medicine for all of us." He banged around the kitchen until he located the teapot and three cups.

Lucy laughed. A blind person could see her father wasn't comfortable in the kitchen. "Fill the pot with water and set it on the stove to boil. The tea leaves are in that cabinet. I can finish things from that point."

"Thank you, daughter." He muttered something about a woman's job being complicated, but eventually got the pot on the stove. "I'm stepping outside for a breath of … dirty air."

The wind caught the door and banged it against the wall. "We've got a package." Papa carried something flat wrapped in brown paper, inside. "It has Lucy's name on it."

"Open it for me, please."

He ripped off the wrapping. "It's your sketches."

Jack had brought them and left. Now, she had no reason to seek him out. Her spirits fell. Mama would never allow her to pay him a visit without a good reason.

Perhaps it was for the best. At least for now. Mama's heart needed a lot of tenderizing before she would accept Lucy's friendship with Jack.

~

The next morning, Jack walked barefoot through a surf more active than in days past. His heart leaped as he spotted Lucy coming from the opposite direction. While his head told him to turn around and keep his distance, his traitorous heart caused his steps to increase, bringing him closer to her.

"You came." He stopped just inches from her and gazed into her face.

"I don't have much time. Mama will be looking for me, but I wanted to thank you for bringing my drawings last night."

"You're welcome. I know how much they mean to you."

The wind teased the strands of her hair, sending them across her face, as the waves soaked the hem of her skirt. He didn't make mention of the few drawings he saw she had done of him. Knowing she cared enough to capture his likeness was enough.

"Are you going to the volcano today?" She raised her amazing eyes to his.

"I wanted to, but I fear it's too dangerous. Perhaps if we didn't go all the way to the crater?"

"We?"

"If you can get away."

"Oh, Jack. What are we doing?" Her eyes shimmered with unshed tears. "Not only do we risk our lives to see a spectacle that could kill us, but I risk my mother's wrath if we continue to try and find ways to see each other. I fear we're headed down a fool's path." She ducked her head. "My parents want to leave the island at the end of the year. I will do everything in my power to stay behind, but you've made it clear how the islanders feel about foreigners. Why torture ourselves for something that has so much against it?"

"So, you've come to say goodbye." His heart sank.

"While it rips my heart to say so, I think it's for the best. At least for now. I have work to do convincing my mother that I know what is best for me." Her tears escaped, rolling down her cheeks.

He knew better than to care for a woman. Love brought only heartache, and here he was, experiencing it without any declarations of love. He stepped back. "As you wish." He spun and marched away, ignoring her calls of his name.

The ocean at their feet increased its ferocity, warning them of a tumultuous day ahead. How fitting that the surroundings matched the turmoil in his heart. The day, darkened by the ash cloud, matched his mood. Rather than heading home, he continued his trek down the beach.

He thought he heard Lucy call his name again, the wind tossing it out to sea. Instead of turning, he increased his speed, running along the sand in a vain attempt to outrun his pain. Why hadn't he kept to his resolve not to care again?

He raced past a group of tourists who had elected to stay and watch the volcano's deadly actions. At least they were watching from a safe distance. Winded, legs aching from running in the wet sand, he collapsed on a sand dune and stared at a gray sea.

A glance to his left showed Lucy making her way toward him. She'd said her piece, why wouldn't she leave him alone?

She stopped next to him, her face stained from her tears. "Please, don't leave angry with me.

You're the only friend I have on this island."

"I can't be your friend." Jack pushed to his feet. "What will your mother say?"

"Please, don't do this." She reached out a hand. "My intent wasn't to push you away, but to ask you to see our ... relationship ... through the eyes of others."

"We don't have a relationship." He stepped out of her reach. "I will work with you through this disaster, but as colleagues with a common goal, nothing more." He turned and strode away.

The stubborn girl ran to catch up with him. "You're being ridiculous. We're two adults."

"Tell that to your mother." He stopped and closed his eyes, regretting his biting words. "I'm sorry. Let me be, Lucy."

The ground shook under his feet. "Go home," he told her. "You aren't safe out here." The height of the waves increased, soaking him to the knees. "Your hut will be enough to protect you."

"Not if the shaking grows in strength. I'm safer on open ground."

True, but he didn't want to be responsible for her when the volcano blew. "I need to find my aunt." He took a step past her.

The ground groaned, throwing him to his knees. A gigantic explosion filled the air, shooting an ash cloud high into the air.

Lucy shrieked.

Jack crawled toward her and shielded her with his body, hoping, praying, they wouldn't be engulfed by waves caused by the volcano's eruption. He headed further on shore, dragging

Lucy after him. Sea water dripped from their hair and clothes.

So blinded had he been while sinking into despair, he hadn't paid enough attention to his surroundings. The ash fell heavier, blocking out the already weak sun. The temperature dropped, causing him to shiver.

He glanced up as the volcano spewed flaming rocks and magma into the air, lighting that portion of the sky with crimson and black. He closed his eyes and pulled Lucy closer. She cried out as he hit against her shoulder.

"Shhh," he whispered as she shuddered. "We're fine here. We'll only be wet and dirty." He spotted her parents standing on the lanai of their hut. "Come on. Your parents are looking for you."

They struggled to their feet. Against a ground that refused to remain steady under them, Jack helped her to her parents. He gave her father a nod, and left, heading toward his own hut without a backward glance.

6

Lucy coaxed her parents into the open and watched the display over the volcano. The ash cloud seemed to reach heaven, shooting out flaming rocks and fiery liquid. Mama gasped with each new explosion.

Jack, hands shoved deep in his pockets, shuffled past them. Lucy followed him like a woman starved. While she knew not pursuing a relationship with him at the moment was for the best, her heart ached with a pain that might never heal. How could she feel so strongly for a man she had known for only a few weeks?

"Don't worry." Papa drew her into an embrace. "Everything will work out. Relax and watch God's fury from a safe place."

She leaned into his shoulder, grateful for his gentle love. Papa draped his other arm around Mama and the three stood in rapturous wonder as the day was cast into further darkness, and the mountain caught fire.

"I want to go up there when this is over," she said. "I want to see the changes."

Papa chuckled. "At least you said when it's

over. You'll be the death of me, daughter. But, I understand your fascination."

"There will be many who will need our help," Mama said, her voice barely above a whisper. "This ash will block the sun for days. Food will be ruined. The task before us is daunting."

"We're up to it." Papa rested his chin on her head.

Would Lucy ever find a love like the one her parents had? She glanced in the direction of Jack's home, not surprised to see him and his aunt staying out front, their gazes locked on the volcano. The other huts were eerily empty, the residents having fled the day before. How many would come home after the eruption?

Mama was right. Food and water would be scarce. Lucy straightened. She would do her part to minister both physically and spiritually. If they all worked as a community, they would survive this disaster.

Lucy's hair stood on end seconds before a torrential downpour fell from the clouds overhead. She dashed, along with her parents, for the protection of the hut. It seemed the worst of the explosions were over. Her family was safe, as was Jack. Her spirit calmed as she watched mud fall from the sky.

She sat on the threadbare sofa to change from her slippers to her boots as Papa stepped back outside. There would be no traipsing up the mountain in flimsy footwear. Oh, how she wished she could borrow a pair of Papa's trousers.

"Lucy." Papa shook his hair like a wet dog.

Mama scolded as mud dotted the floor. "I've fetched Mr. Garrison to escort you up the mountain."

Lucy's heart leaped.

"I trust no one else to keep you safe. He has proven his worth many times over." Papa leaned close. "I only caution you to guard your heart. Nothing more than friendship can exist between the two of you."

As quickly as her heart had rejoiced, it despaired. Papa only cared about her physical well-being. Why couldn't her parents see where her heart lay and be happy?

She tied her laces, grabbed her drawing supplies, and headed outside to greet a stony faced Jack. He handed her a wide-brimmed hat and a bandanna.

"You'll need this if you plan on not dying of asphyxiation or being covered in mud. It will filter the air." He marched to the makeshift barn.

Lucy tugged off her sling, wanting as much arm mobility as possible, and slogged after him. It was going to be a long, silent day if Jack's cool shoulder was any indication. Still, he had come at her father's request. She would be happy with whatever time she had with him.

Without a word, he helped her into the mare's saddle, mounted his own horse, and led the way away from the string of huts. Lucy sighed and fell in behind him, trying not to focus on Jack's rigidness and instead on the majestic cloud rising in the distance.

The closer they got, the more boulders, one

weighing at least three hundred pounds, blocked the path. Others rose above the lava flow. The air, cool down below, was hot the closer they got to the crater.

Jack stopped. "The horses stay here." He slid from the saddle and untied a bag he had stuck behind his saddle. "We'll have lunch at the top and you can draw."

"Won't you talk to me?" She put a hand on his arm, stopping him.

"I think you've said all that needs to be said." He stared straight ahead, a muscle ticking in his jaw.

"You're the one who said an islander can't get involved with someone from the mainland. Your words, not mine." Her blood boiled. "I only asked for time, Jack, not for eternity."

He sighed. "I don't know what I want." He cast pain-filled eyes on her. "You've shaken every resolution I've ever made." He took a deep breath under his bandanna. "You and this volcano have spun my world out of control. I don't like that."

"It isn't something I can help." Or change. Perspiration dripped from her brow. Falling ash stuck to her skin. Instead of the adventurous day she had wanted, she got an uncomfortable one with a surly companion.

She felt a large rock to make sure it wasn't too hot, sat down, and opened her sketch pad. She could wile away the hours by drawing and leave Jack to his unpleasantness.

The ground trembled slightly under her feet. She glanced at the crater, which had partially collapsed. When no further explosions erupted, she turned back to her drawing. The landscape had changed drastically since the day before, and she wanted to capture as much as possible on paper. Of course, she'd heard of several photographers visiting the site, but the drawings were as much for her as for others.

Mr. Woodward, and a man Lucy didn't know, climbed the mountain. "Quite a show!"

"Yes, sir, it was." Lucy grinned under her face cloth.

"The military base took quite a few hits from falling rocks," he said. "It looks like a bomb went off. A few soldiers are missing, but the civilians were evacuated before the major eruption." He pulled a handkerchief from his pocket and mopped his brow before tying it around his nose and mouth. He directed the younger man to take some samples from the area around the crater.

"I must admit I wasn't surprised to see you here, sketching away. Nor was I surprised to see Mr. Garrison accompanying you. You two are as fervent in your inquisitiveness as any scientists I've ever met."

"I will take that as a compliment." Lucy returned to sketching the mouth of the crater, making sure to draw in Jack's form as he peered into a crevice. It felt good to be appreciated.

"Are you ready to eat?" Jack pulled her attention away from her work. "It's simple sandwiches, but ought to keep you from starving."

"Any food is good food." She closed her pad. "I fear many will go hungry in the coming days."

Jack handed her a ham sandwich wrapped in leaves and squatted next to her. "Some of the crevices seem bottomless, and the amount of power it took to hurl rocks the size of some of them cast from the crater is mind boggling."

"I know it wasn't possible, but imagine the excitement of having been here, in this spot, when the volcano blew." She could only imagine.

"I think there were a few who experienced it first hand, from what Mr. Woodward is saying."

Lucy racked her brain for something else to say. At least Jack was talking, even if it was only about the day's events and nothing personal. "What are your plans over the next few days?"

"I need to check on my cattle." He stood and brushed crumbs from his pant legs. "I'd hate to lose any."

"Surely, they were safe where you had them corralled."

He nodded. "Most likely, but I'd like to see first hand. Hopefully, none of them got spooked and escaped the hasty pen we erected." He held out a hand. "We'd better head back. I promised your father we wouldn't be gone long."

"Will I see you on the beach tomorrow?"

~

He wanted to say no, but knew the futility of the lie. He would be there, heartache or not, if only to catch a glimpse of her face. It seemed that he, Jack Garrison, professed bachelor, had been ensnared by the very type of woman he had sworn to stay away from.

They made the ride home in silence, same as

they had left. While Lucy hurried to her hut, Jack took care of the mare before riding his own horse to his temporary cattle ranch.

"Boss!" His foreman, Manuel Okymoto, rushed toward him. "Come see. It's a mad house."

Jack handed the horse's reins to a waiting drover and followed the foreman. They crested a small rise. His heart stopped. It seemed the entire village had decided to set up camp among his cattle. "How many are gone?"

"Twenty-five head at the count after the explosions quit. When the people arrived, the fences were weakened and the explosions set the cattle into a stampede."

Jack swallowed against the dryness in his throat. "Was anyone injured?"

Manuel shook his head. "But the grass is trampled and the water muddied. What are we going to do?"

"Have you told the crowd they can head back to their huts?"

"They won't listen. One man said that since the cattle were safe here, they would be, too."

Jack groaned. He couldn't care for all these people. "Send someone to the missionary. Tell him what has happened and see what advice he has." Mr. Dillow had ministered to these very people for months. Hopefully, he would know what to do.

Striving to show much more authority than he felt, Jack headed for the center of the camp. While he didn't own the land he had corralled his cattle on, he hoped the people would see reason. Their camping in the area put his cattle at risk, not to mention the young children who raced around. If the cattle were to stampede again, he couldn't bear for anyone to be trampled. He should have left the herd at the ranch and taken his chances there. They'd be no better off than they were now.

"Manuel! Find the lost cattle and send them home."

"Are you sure, boss? The ash is thicker there, the air more fowl."

Jack shook is head. His foreman was right. They were all stuck here for the duration.

He made the rounds, pleading with the people to leave, telling them the beachfront huts were safe. They refused to move again, several said. A creek provided running water, and a nearby pineapple plantation gave them fresh fruit. Several eyed his cattle, stating a need for fresh meat. Not a chance. The cattle were his livelihood.

Resigned to the fact that he, too, must move, Jack headed back to the beach to inform Anake they would be roughing it in a tent.

"No." She crossed her arms. "I am staying here."

"If you stay, then I have to travel back and forth every day for meals."

"That is your choice." She stomped inside the hut.

"Anake, please. I can't take care of you and my cattle with an hour's ride each way." Why were women so stubborn?

"I can take care of myself." She turned and put her hands on his cheeks. "I love you. You're my boy. But I am too old to live in a tent."

Jack stifled a groan. Everything was falling apart around him, literally. "I'll ride back and forth."

She patted his cheek. "Do what you must. I'll fix you some dinner to take back with you."

He stepped outside to spot the other thorn, uh, woman, in his side as she and her family loaded a small hand cart with household goods. "Heading to the camp?"

"That is where we are needed," Mr. Dillow said.

From the look on Mrs. Dillow's face, she wasn't happy with the idea. Lucy smiled timidly at him, clearly not distressed over the change in living conditions. The girl was of stout material, despite her petite frame. She was even using her shoulder to lift things into the cart.

Jack rushed forward. "You should be letting your shoulder heal."

"It's only a little tender. I can't let it keep me from doing what is needed."

"We've work to do, Mr. Garrison," her mother stated. "Unless you have a better idea for helping us move, other than talking, then you had better leave."

"I could try to find a wagon." He cocked his head. Why couldn't she be more civil? It must be so difficult to embrace each day with such bitterness.

He smiled at Lucy, tipped his hat at her father, and headed down the street to find a wagon. With so many fleeing the area after the explosion, all he could find was a lopsided hand a cart. Still, it was better than nothing. He tightened a loose wheel and pushed it to the Dillows.

"It isn't much, but it will lessen what you carry on your backs."

"Bless you, Mr. Garrison." Mr. Dillow clapped him on the back. "Now, try to talk sense into my daughter. She is insisting on carrying a fifty pound pack on her back."

"Papa!" Lucy's face darkened. "I'm perfectly capable."

"Of carrying something half your weight?" Jack took the pack and slung it over his shoulder. "Anake will take a strap to me if you re-injure yourself. Save my hide by letting me carry this."

"Very well." She sighed and shook her head, grabbing a smaller satchel. "Is it all right with you if I carry this in my good hand?"

He laughed, admiring her spirit. "Whatever makes you happy."

He strolled until he was in front of her parents and led them to his pasture land which crawled with more people than cattle.

"Boss." Manuel raced to Jack's side. "There are a group of people trying to steal one of our calves for food. I'm outnumbered."

So, it began. Jack tossed the pack he carried on top of the overflowing handcart, tossed an apologetic glance at the Dillows, and dashed after his foreman.

"Hey." He yanked a lead rope out of a man's hand. "These cattle belong to me."

"My children are hungry."

"Then hunt the forest for fruit. You can't steal from me. This is my livelihood."

The man planted his fists on his hips. "But it is okay for me to steal from the man who owns the pineapple field? Or the sugar cane?"

"No, but—" Jack glanced around the crowd. Most of them still wore ash in their hair and on their clothes. One small calf wouldn't go far. How much more would they want? "The sea is full of fish. The flounder is easy enough to catch."

"With this many?" The man waved an arm. "The beach would soon be clear of seaweed and the flounder gone. We need your beef."

"Out of the question." Rope in hand, Jack led the calf back to his mother.

He wanted to help the people, he did, but he couldn't give up a valuable calf in order to feed the people for a day. They knew how to fish. Didn't the bible say something about a man that knew how to fish would always have food?

"Surely there is something you can do?"

He turned to stare at Lucy. "Like what?"

"Don't you have an old cow or something that is no longer valuable?" She peered up at him, her hazel eyes wide. "In a time like this, we must all work together. Those who have much must share with those who don't."

"I'd like to help, but I can't make myself poor just to feed people for a day."

"Just so my father has time to organize things. Once we're settled, he'll assign tasks for fishing and hunting. Someone can find the chickens that scattered from the village. We only need your help for one day, Jack. How can you be so selfish?"

7

How could she have been so wrong about Jack? Lucy blinked back tears. It took a disaster to show a man's true colors. Still, his willingness to help her and her family had led her to believe he was a compassionate, caring person. Now, his selfishness threatened to overshadow everything she had believed about him.

"One cow, Jack," she said. "That's all we're asking."

He closed his eyes, shook his head, and walked away. She headed back to help her father set up the patched tent that had seen so many better days.

"I told you these were not our people," Mama said, pounding in a stake at the corner of the tent. "You'll spare yourself a lot of grief by remembering that."

"We're here to minister to the island's inhabitants. That's what I choose to remember." Lucy hefted a hammer, the effort pulling at her burned shoulder. She would have to find another way to help.

She unloaded her family's bedding and did her best to shake the ash from the blankets. Within minutes she was as gray as the hair on Papa's head.

"Lucy! Shake those somewhere else." Mama glared. "You're causing as much damage as the volcano."

A military truck rumbled to a stop next to them, raising another cloud of dust and ash. Mama sighed and marched into the now erected tent.

"We're looking for the missionary," the driver said. "Would you be Mr. Dillow?"

"I am." Papa wiped his hands on his trousers and extended one.

The driver, a young man not much older than Lucy, returned the shake. "We've supplies in the back. Not a lot, but they will help you feed these people for a week or so, if rationed."

"God bless you." Papa beamed. "See, daughter, God does supply our needs."

The soldier glanced appreciatively in Lucy's direction. She turned her back and carried the blankets into the tent. She didn't want the attention of any man other than Jack, and since that seemed to be going nowhere, she would continue teaching the native children and leave the rest up to God.

In fact, she'd start right away. She unpacked her teaching supplies and quickly wrote several fliers stating she would begin classes again in the morning next to the giant hibiscus bush at the west end of the meadow. Her life might be upside down, but that didn't mean she shouldn't do what she had come to the island to do.

"I'm going to distribute fliers about restarting school, Mama." Lucy slid her supplies under her cot.

"I'm glad to hear your head is back where it

belongs." Mama snapped a sheet in place over another cot.

Lucy bit her tongue and ducked out of the tent. Papa opened the crates deposited in front of the tent, the grin on his face spreading.

"What a bounty," he said, tossing Lucy a pineapple. "Hand that to your mother to go with our lunch."

Lucy returned his smile, set the fruit inside the tent, and made her way through the camp, informing the families of her students about the restart of school. She hung her last flier on a fence post and watched as Jack, on horseback, guided three of his cattle into a makeshift corral. His hair, worn longer than most people deemed respectable, blew around his face. He was truly one of God's masterpieces. If only his heart was as honorable as Lucy had once thought.

She remained where she was as he slid from his saddle and handed the reins to a native man in western clothes. Jack marched to where a family with several small children struggled to erect a tent, and helped them get their temporary home ready.

Perhaps he wasn't as uncaring as he had seemed earlier. Lucy understood not wanting to destroy one's livelihood, but she still didn't understand his unwillingness to share his fortune. Maybe time would soften his heart.

With an hour to spare before lunch, she headed for the beach, a longer walk than when they lived in the cottages. But, if she walked fast, she would have half an hour to enjoy the surf and waves. The sea calmed her spirit better than anything else.

She toed off her boots, hitched her skirt up around her knees, and waded into the surf. Seaweed caressed her legs. She knew the islanders ate the sea vegetable, but didn't know which were safe. She unwrapped a strand from her ankle and studied it. It all looked the same to her.

"Don't eat that," Jack said from behind her. "That is not native to the island. Here." He pointed to a mat-like seaweed, yellowish in appearance. "This is lima. See the way it has yellowed in the sun? Over here, in the shade, it looks red or dark brown."

Lucy dropped the slimy stuff in her hand and went to where he stood. "We eat this as a vegetable," he explained. "In fact, your father is assigning some of the women the task of collecting this each morning to include with the communal meals. Others will head to the mountains for mountain apples and guava."

"Since you are so knowledgeable," she said, "you could lead the groups."

"All the natives know what is safe to eat and what are not." He stared across the ocean. "I will help build boxes to hunt for flounder this evening. I'm doing what I can, Lucy. There is no sense in killing one of my cattle when other food is waiting in plenty." He gazed down at her. "Would you like to go octopus hunting one night? A good sized one will feed several people."

"That sounds like fun. Are we going tonight?"

He laughed. "If you'd like. I have an extra spear you can use. I'll pick you up at sundown."

"I'll bring a flashlight." Her heart leaped,

knowing she would be spending time with Jack. Not only that, but he was going to teach her some about being self-sufficient in his land. More each day, she grew close to becoming one with the people she loved. Now, to convince Mama of the importance of meeting Jack to learn how to hunt octopus.

"I'll see you then." He turned and walked away.

Not their usual time spent on the beach together, but it was better than nothing. She lowered her skirt, scandalized that Jack had most likely seen way more of her legs than was proper. Still, he hadn't batted an eye. She slipped her boots on her wet feet, grabbed a handful of the safe-to-eat seaweed, and dashed toward the tent to prepare the groundwork with her mother for later that evening.

"Absolutely not." Mama crossed her arms.

"That is, without a doubt, your favorite phrase where I'm concerned." Lucy sat on an overturned crate. "Papa, help her see the wisdom in letting me learn what is safe to eat here."

"She has a point, dear." Papa hacked a coconut in half. "This island paradise is full of bounty. It is in her best interest to know which foods are safe."

"Then I insist she have a chaperone."

"Mama!" Lucy took a deep breath and struggled to control her temper. "Mr. Garrison has been nothing but a gentleman. He is the best teacher I could have. If you wish to accompany us, getting wet in the process, then you are welcome to come. But," Lucy lifted her chin, "I will insist that you participate."

"I detest the ocean."

Which Lucy knew very well and was counting on. "Then I will go alone with Mr. Garrison and bring back tomorrow's dinner. I'm sure there will be others hunting as well." The refugees were always present. Lucy would be very safe.

~

Ignoring the glares from Mrs. Dillow, Jack handed Lucy a small three-pronged spear and escorted her, along with several others wanting to get in on the fun, to the beach. Lucy's flashlight illuminated the path ahead of them as everyone talked and laughed as if heading to a party.

Lucy seemed to have forgiven Jack for whatever infraction he had caused by not butchering his cattle, and almost skipped at his side. He shoved aside the urge to wrap his arm around her waist and let everyone around them know his true feelings for the spirited woman next to him.

Until he won over her parents, and Lucy was no longer considered a foreigner, that could never happen. But, Jack Garrison was a patient man. He had a few months left to win over the Dillow family.

The villagers scattered, headed to their favorite hunting places. With his hand on the small of her back, Jack guided Lucy down the shore to where several rocky reefs stuck above the water.

"Look for places where it seems small rocks and shells have been misplaced." He took the light from her hand and shined it around the area. "The octopus hide during this time, but will have dug into their home. If you think you have found a spot, stab your spear into the hole and tug. They won't make it easy."

Her eyes widened. "Won't that hurt them?"

"You're going to eat them, right?"

She giggled. "I suppose it doesn't matter at this point, does it?"

He smiled. "Not really."

"I'm ready." She marched ahead, searching the jagged rocks for anyplace an octopus might choose as its home for the night.

The moon cast a silver glow on her dark hair. Her white blouse seemed to glow in the dark in direct contrast with the darker skirt she wore. He didn't think he could ever tire of looking at her. As her bare feet left impressions in the sand, she looked like a fairy tale creature on land for only the night. He planned on enjoying every minute of the time they had.

"In here!" Lucy squatted, unmindful of the water, in front of a hole in the rocks. "See how the area is disturbed?"

"Stick in your spear."

She squared her shoulders and shoved. "How will I know if I have one?"

"It will feel squishy. A rock won't."

"Eew." She jabbed harder, then yanked, falling backward into the water, fully submerging herself. She came up sputtering, spear in hand. At the end of the prongs wiggled an octopus Jack guessed to weigh around three pounds.

"Very good." He laughed and helped her stand.

The moonlight illuminated her eyes, causing him to lose all reason. Without thinking, he pulled her close and kissed her. His pulse soared to the moon. When she didn't immediately pull free, he deepened the kiss, wrapping his arm around her waist and holding her still. When she made a sound deep in her throat, he released her.

"Congratulations."

She ducked her head. "Is that the reward for every octopus I catch?"

"Do you want it to be?"

She stared into his face. "I don't know."

She handed him the spear so he could remove her catch and drop it into the bag hanging at his waist. She kept her head down, but not before he saw the smile teasing the corners of her mouth "Let's look for more."

So, she wanted to act as if the kiss didn't happen. His spirit fell. He could pretend, but he wouldn't forget. Obviously her earlier statement about wanting to marry an islander in order to stay no longer rang true. She seemed to be mentally preparing herself to leave the island. Still, there was the shy smile she had tried to hide. He chose to hold on to that as a sliver of hope.

The hair on the back of his neck prickled. He glanced over his shoulder to see the form of a woman watching from a rise. Mrs. Dillow, no doubt. She had most likely seen him kiss her daughter and was already forming consequences in her mind.

Why did she dislike him so much? It had to be more than his native blood. After all, she had come hundreds of miles in order to minister to his people. Jack was an upstanding member of the community, wealthy in his own right, and tried to do right by those around him. Yes, his faith had faltered after losing his family and the woman he loved to the sea, but that couldn't be her only reason for thinking him unworthy of her only child. He needed a plan. Win over the mother, and he would win the heart of the daughter.

He increased his pace to catch up with Lucy, who poked her spear into another hole. "Got something?"

"I think so." She yanked out her spear, keeping her footing this time, and pulled out a long eel. She screamed and dropped the spear.

Jack leaped forward before she was bitten. "It's only a baby one." Using his boot, he released the offending creature and let it make its way back home.

From the shouts of glees down the beach, others were also catching food. The refugees wouldn't go hungry the next day. Once the sea life on their portion of the island was depleted, they would have to forage farther away, and Jack would have to reconsider giving up one of his cattle. He would, gladly, if he saw a genuine reason to do so. But, that wouldn't happen until there was no other recourse.

He put his fingers in his mouth and gave a shrill whistle to call everyone back. There was no need to catch more than they could eat at one sitting.

"I only caught one." Lucy sloshed to his side.

"You'll do better next time." He took her spear, adding it to his, which he hadn't used, and led the way up the embankment. Mrs. Dillow no longer stared down with her icy glare.

"I think your mother saw us kiss," he said.

"You mean she saw you kiss me." Lucy kicked at a loose rock, sending it into the shallow water.

"You returned the kiss." He stopped and faced her. "Or was I mistaken in feeling the passion of your lips against mine?"

"I'd rather not talk about it." She glanced up the hill. "Mama will lecture me for hours."

He wanted to ask her whether it was worth the consequences. Instead, he continued his trek back to camp. Lucy may regret the kiss now, but he doubted she would forget.

"Goodnight. You did well. Tomorrow, I'll take you into the forest and teach you which fruits and nuts are safe to consume."

"Thank you." She flashed a smile, gathered her skirts in her hands, and dashed toward her tent.

Jack joined the others who were successful at catching octopus, and tossed Lucy's catch into a barrel of rainwater. Ten good size octopus would feed everyone for two or three meals.

He wasn't sure why he felt responsible for those camping in his north pasture, but he did. Very much so. Mr. Dillow probably felt the same. At the first opportunity, Jack would speak with the missionary and see whether they could work together until the ash cleared and folks could salvage what was left of their homes.

He studied the area. Two weeks at the most, and they could all return home. He missed Anake. Since he had established boundaries, as far as his cattle went, he headed for the cottage, determined to sleep under a solid roof. He grinned. He'd fall asleep thinking of Lucy's kiss and how she had looked in the moonlight.

8

"One man gives freely, yet gains even more; another withholds unduly, but comes to poverty." Papa closed his Bible. "That is from Proverbs 11:24. Not only are we to give in times such as this, but we are to ask when we are in need."

Lucy fiddled with the ribbon around her throat. Papa's words made sense, of course, coming from God's Word. She could only pray they would fall on the hearts of those listening. While most of the islanders were extravagant with their giving, they hesitated to ask when in need themselves. Food was in short supply. Thankfully, they would all be able to return home soon. Jack and a few of the other men were heading to the village after the church service to determine the safety of returning home.

It'd been a week since the eruption and the sun was once again showing its face upon the island. Lucy's fingers itched to head to the crater and draw the changes that had occurred during that time. But, Mama had kept Lucy firmly by her side since the night of octopus hunting. The imprisonment was stifling. She had even been forced to hold school right outside their tent.

Mama treated her like a child. She expelled air sharply through her nose and tried to concentrate on what Papa was saying. A sharp elbow in the rib cage from Mama for fidgeting didn't help. Nor did the fact that Jack leaned against a palm tree and watched the service from under the brim of his hat.

Lucy sat on her hands to keep from running her forefinger over her lips. Even after three days, she could feel his lips on hers.

"What is wrong with you?" Mama frowned. "You're acting like a toddler who has to sit too long."

"I'm sorry." She tried to focus, she really did, but the beautiful day and the smoking mountain in the distance called to her.

She was tired of drawing flowers and shells. She snuck another peek at Jack. Her sketch book was filled with pictures she had drawn of him as he worked around the camp. Pictures of him on horseback or fishing. She would definitely add the image of him leaning against the tree to her portfolio.

Mama caught her looking. "Stop your infatuation with that man this instant. Oh, it is a good thing we are leaving in a few months. You worry me."

After service, the community gathered in a common area where several of the women who had no desire to learn more about the white man's god, cooked a large meal of rice wrapped in leaves.

Lucy loved the sweet treat and took her lunch to the shade of a hibiscus bush. Jack nodded, his eyes smoldering under his hat, and marched to fetch his food. She half expected him to come sit with her, but when Mama spread a blanket next to her, he swerved and joined several men next to the corral.

She didn't know another nineteen-year-old woman who had such a consistent chaperone. She laid her food on her lap. "Mama, I'm going to the volcano to sketch this afternoon."

"No."

"I want to see how things have changed. Mr. Woodward should be by any day now to see if I have anything new."

"He is busy at the military base and doesn't have time for the foolish whims of a young girl." Mama wiped her fingers on a monogramed handkerchief.

Even in the aftermath of disaster, she always looked cool and collected. How did she do it? Lucy always seemed to be covered in dust, her hair falling from the bun at the nape of her neck. Even Papa usually looked rumpled.

"Sundays are my own. You've said it many times, and I choose to spend it at the volcano." Lucy crushed the leaves that had been wrapped around her rice and tossed it into a pail carried by a young boy. "I'm an adult, and I wish you would stop treating me as a child. Your old-fashioned ideas are creating a wedge between us. I want to be your friend, Mama."

"I'm your mother, not your friend." Her eyes shimmered.

"Yes, but I don't need the structure I once needed as a child." Why couldn't she see how much Lucy desired for things to be better between them?

She loved her mother dearly, but also wanted to spread her wings and find her own way in the world.

"You have wounded me deeply. I am retiring to our tent." Mama pushed to her feet and marched away.

Lucy's heart ached. She hadn't meant to hurt her, only to express her feelings. Mama didn't need to be so dramatic. She needed her own interests, something to bring her joy. Her clothing designs! Lucy jumped up and barged into the tent.

"I have a gift for you, Mama." She dug in a trunk under her cot, pulling out a fresh sketch pad. Her last one.

"I have a headache. A gift will not undo the harm you've done to me."

"Please, stop." Lucy set the pad on her mother's lap and added a lead pencil. "I want to see some of your designs. I need a new dress."

"I don't have time for such foolishness."

"You don't do anything on Sundays, other than nap. You have all afternoon." Lucy patted her mother's hand, then stepped back out into the sunshine.

Half an hour later, having talked one of Jack's men into saddling the little mare, Lucy headed for the mountain. Dead vegetation, seared from the volcano's heat, lay withered and brown under several inches of ash. Boulders as big as the horse lay tossed around like a child's toy blocks. The area was void of life, the air still carrying a tinge of sulphur smell. Thin rivers of lava flowed toward the sea.

Lucy tethered the mare halfway up the volcano, then walked the rest of the way. The poor beast would have little to nibble on. She would sketch a quick rough draft of the crater and its surroundings, then head for home.

Her drawing took longer than planned, and the sun hung low over the horizon before Lucy headed for home. While she had kept a look out for Jack, hoping against reason that he would discover where she had gone and follow, she hadn't got one glimpse of him. Disappointment filled her, despite the peace of the day. Had she forgotten how to exist without his presence?

For years she had been content with teaching and drawing. Then, she had caught her glimpse of the islands and the handsome Paniolo who rode a big horse. The man's eyes were as stormy and deep as the sea, and his hair as luxurious as a seal. She chuckled. She sounded like a love struck poet. What would Mama say?

She arrived home to see her mother bent over the sketch pad, the pencil flying across the paper as she sketched. Lucy's heart warmed as she led the mare to the stable and handed her over to one of the workers.

So deep was Mama involved in what she was doing, she looked up startled when Lucy stopped next to her. "You mustn't sneak up on me like that."

Lucy peered down. A gown, its train spread around the hem, fairly leaped from the page. Pearls covered a high bodice. "It's beautiful."

"It's how I imagine your wedding dress to be one day." Mama beamed up at her. "Thank you. I desperately needed this."

"I would be proud to get married in something that fine." Lucy sat next to her.

"How did your drawing go?"

Mama was actually showing interest! "The area is much changed. So barren and void of life. Very depressing, really, but I think I captured the violence of the volcano." Making sure to skip over any drawings of Jack, except the ones of him staring into the crater, she showed her mother every scene she had sketched, from the first to the one that day.

"You're very talented. I can envision the power and majesty of what had happened up there."

"I must get my talent from my mother." Lucy rested her head against her mother's shoulder, wishing she could capture the moment on paper.

Several villagers strolled by shouting, "Aloha."

Lucy smiled and returned the greeting, thinking once again how much at home she felt. She wanted to help Mama understand, but wouldn't do anything to ruin the moment of tenderness between them.

"I'd best be seeing what we have to contribute to the community pot." Mama stood. "Supplies are running low, but I did hear the military got in a shipload of supplies yesterday. The shops should be well stocked when we head home. I've heard we may be able to go home as early as Tuesday."

"Where is Papa?"

"He is speaking with Mr. Garrison about checking the village for safety."

~

"If we are prepared to examine the village in the morning," Mr. Dillow said, "we will know whether everyone can return home. I'm sure that will please you greatly."

"It will be nice to have my cattle back where grazing is plentiful." Jack leaned his back against the corral fence and propped a boot on a rail. "Your sermon this morning was ... enlightening."

"Oh?" Mr. Dillow glanced up from where he mended a corner of a neighbor's tent. "Which part? Helping others or asking for help?"

"The part about a lukewarm faith." Jack studied a blade of grass struggling to grow in the packed soil. "I never lost mine after the death of my family, but I have faltered. Your simple words this morning helped me realize that."

"I'm glad to know I helped." He straightened and wiped his hands on his already stained trousers. "There is something else I would like to speak with you about." He glanced to where Lucy tossed a pail of dirty water into a bush.

Jack's mouth dried up. He knew what the man was going to say before he uttered a word.

"You're a good man, Mr. Garrison. One of the best. But I'd like to request that you stop toying with my daughter's affections."

"Toying is nowhere close to how I feel about her, sir." Jack clenched his fists and shoved them into his pockets.

"She is young and impressionable. Her mother has higher aspirations for Lucy than this island can give her."

"I have the means for Lucy to live like royalty." Jack bit back the harsh words he wanted to say in his defense. "I've the money to take her to the mainland a couple of times a year for the culture you and Mrs. Dillow seem to think she needs."

Mr. Dillow held up a hand to stop him. "I have no worries about the lifestyle you can give her. Please don't misunderstand me. My concern is that my daughter would never truly be accepted here. She is tolerated, as the children's teacher, and possibly more liked than myself or my wife, but she is still a haole. Nothing can change that."

"My father was not a native and he became very well loved." Jack pushed away from the fence. Pain ripped through him like a tidal wave. "At first, I thought and felt the same as you, but the more I came to know Lucy, I realized how wrong I was. She lives with her heart, Mr. Dillow. She will be accepted no matter where she goes in life."

"See that woman there?" He pointed to Ana, the daughter of the island's king. "She is beautiful, island royalty, and a native. Doesn't it make more sense for you to cast your attentions in her direction?"

"Ana is a spoiled, willful child." Jack stomped away, no longer caring what the man thought of him. He glanced at the darkening sky. He'd cast his feelings on a man who couldn't see past the nose on his face. So much for wanting to deepen his faith. Not to mention his desire to leave behind bachelorhood after years of saying he'd never marry.

He watched as Ana sashayed past him, her dark eyes issuing an invitation he didn't want to accept. Still, maybe Mr. Dillow had a point. If they would not accept Jack as a suitor for their daughter, it might behoove him to look elsewhere for his bride. He pasted on a grin and walked Ana to his family's tent, trying not to roll his eyes at her non-ending chatter regarding the latest fashions on the mainland. Perhaps he should look at a less lofty girl. One that didn't exhaust his brain with nonsense.

Lucy carried a lantern outside her tent and froze when she caught a glimpse of him with Ana. It didn't help when Ana placed a hand on his arm and simpered up at him. Lucy's eyes narrowed in question before she stepped back into the safety of her tent.

His heart fell to his toes. No doubt she was confused to see him with someone else. It couldn't be helped. He couldn't continue to knock on a door that would never be opened for him. He groaned, knowing he would be spending the better part of the next day with her father. While the man was nothing but pleasant toward Jack, now that he knew his true feelings, it would be hard for Jack to keep a civil tongue in his mouth in the face of such prejudice.

The loss of Lucy's companionship ate at him like an insect. He left Ana at her tent, with little more than a curt "goodnight" and headed to the stable to saddle his horse for the ride to his cottage in hopes that Anake would relieve the turmoil in his mind.

She had just finished cleaning the dishes after the simple meal she had cooked for herself. Jack stood in the doorway of the two room cottage and watched. Why couldn't all women be as loving as this dear lady?

Anake turned and gasped. "You startled me. What is wrong, dear?" She rushed toward him and cupped his face. "Who has hurt your heart?"

He wanted to bury his face in her shoulder and cry like the little boy he used to be. As a man, he squared his shoulders and took a deep shuddering breath. "The missionary has asked that I not court his daughter."

"I'm sorry, but you must respect his wishes. Come, I made a cake."

He chuckled. Anake's answers to life's problems was always food. He sat at the rickety wooden table as she placed a cup of coffee and a slice of spice cake in front of him.

"Where did you get the ingredients? They had to have been hard to come by."

"You never mind. We're talking about your girl, not me." Anake joined him. "How does Lucy feel about her father's words?"

"I haven't spoken to her, but I don't think she will agree with her parents." He forked off a bite of the dessert.

"Still, you must respect the father's wishes." Anake crossed her arms. "Is it because of your mother's blood?"

"Yes." His throat clogged despite the cake's moistness. "He fears life would be too hard for her if she was accepted."

Anake made a noise deep in her throat. "Perhaps at one time, but I hear things." She tapped her ear. "That girl is loved by our people. They respect her teaching of the children. If she is the one you want, you must fight for her like a warrior."

He shook his head. "I'm going to transfer my attentions somewhere else. Mr. Dillow is right. Lucy deserves a man who can give her the lifestyle of the mainland."

Anake bolted from her chair and slapped the back of his head. "I never took you for a coward." She stormed from the room and slammed the bedroom door, leaving Jack feeling once again like a child.

He sighed and slid the half-finished cake away. Maybe Mr. Dillow would be more willing to allow Jack to spend time with Lucy if the man saw how hard he worked and how much he cared for the islanders. Tomorrow, Jack would do everything possible to win the man's trust and admiration. He had said Jack was a good man. He would show Mr. Dillow just how good he could be.

Taking his coffee with him, he went to the lanai and sat in a rocking chair. Wait. He recognized the chair as one from the ranch. They hadn't brought it with them when they'd evacuated. Now, the ingredient for the cake made sense. He set his mug on the railing and went to knock on his aunt's door.

"Anake!"

She opened the door and sighed. "Yes, I've gone to the ranch, alone, and brought back some things. It's perfectly safe. We can go home now. You men do things too slowly." She shut the door. "The place needs a good cleaning," she said through the wood. "I will start tomorrow."

Why did no one ever listen to him? He went back to the porch, sat in the rocker, and propped his booted feet on the railing. Lucy didn't listen when he'd expressed his disapproval about her going to the volcano, Mr. Dillow hadn't listened when he'd try to express how he felt about Lucy, and now, Anake hadn't listened about the dangers of heading home without the buildings being checked for safety. Jack might as well talk to one of the boulders thrown from the crater for all the good it did.

He wouldn't be surprised if things went further downhill in the morning with Lucy actually accompanying them into the village. He would not only have to guard his heart from further abuse, but keep an eye on her to keep her safe.

9

"Wait, Papa, I'm coming." Lucy hopped out of the tent, shoving her foot into her boot.

"Checking buildings for safety is no place for a young woman," he said, filling a canteen from a barrel of fresh water.

"I'll be fine. I'm with you." She gave him her most beguiling smile. "I want to see how our home fared. Please, let me go."

He sighed. "I never could deny you." He filled another canteen and handed it to her. "Stay by my side the entire time."

"I will." While not entirely true that he never said no to her wishes, he had a time or two, and no amount of coaxing or whining had changed his mind.

She hung the strap of the canteen around her neck. Would she have time to do any sketches? She decided to leave her pad safely under the mattress of her cot, out of Mama's prying eyes. Their relationship had improved since Mama took up sketching again, but with quite a few of the pictures being of Jack, Lucy wasn't taking any chances.

They trudged through inches of ash until

meeting up with Jack and a handful of other men outside the village where the road had split and fallen a good two feet. Lucy peered into the crack. She couldn't make out anything through the darkness. How deep was it? The road had fallen past the original two feet. Now, there was no depth in sight. Did lava flow just out of sight? She leaned closer. No heart emanated from the crevice.

Taking care to jump over the crack and not trip, she caught up with her father. "I see no reason my daughter cannot accompany us," he said to Jack. "She has a level head on her shoulders and may spot an element of danger we, as men, would overlook."

Jack didn't want her to come? Her shoulders sagged, remembering him strolling with the beautiful Hawaiian girl the night before. How could he have given up on them and moved on? Time would have shown her parents what a good man he was. Why hadn't he waited for her?

No, she'd sent him away. Her. Lucy Dillow and her big mouth about her parents' thoughts. She'd been a coward. Instead of telling Jack how she truly felt, and that she would do everything in her power to convince her parents to get to know him better, she'd pushed him away, rejected his kiss.

The day lost its luster, the sun its cheery warmth. Lucy ducked her head, blinking back tears and refused to enter into the conversation between her father and Jack. Instead, she kicked the dust and ash from a low-lying bush beside the road. She was nothing more than a wishy-washy child who had no idea what she wanted.

She glanced at Jack. Except, she did. She wanted to stay on the island with him. She'd just done such a poor job of showing it, not knowing how much seeing him with someone else would sting. She glared at her father's back. If her parents would treat her as an adult, this entire heartbreak could have been avoided.

The men entered the first building, a small corner store. Lucy chose to stay outside, the thrill of adventure gone from the day.

A jeep full of soldiers rumbled down the road, stopping in front of her. "Hey, pretty lady," the driver said. "What brings you out here alone?"

"She isn't alone." Jack emerged from the store and stood by her side. "We're inspecting the buildings to determine whether the villagers can return home safely."

"Don't get uptight, man. It's our job to question anyone wandering around alone. Looting is against the law." He gave Lucy a big grin, and continued driving down the road.

"Thank you." Lucy squared her shoulders. "But, I'm perfectly capable of taking care of myself. I think I've proven that."

He narrowed his eyes. "Yes, I suppose you have." He turned on a boot heel and stormed back into the store.

What was wrong with her? Here she was, lamenting his lack of attention, and when he plays the hero to protect her from an imagined threat, she shot him down. She leaned against the building and stared at a cloud meandering overhead in a sky the same color as the bluebonnets back home. Lord, she needed some answers.

She sighed and pushed away from the wall. She had come to help, so she might as well get to work. She stepped through the doorway and stopped to let her eyes adjust to the dimness. Shelves were overturned, fabrics and sundries scattered across the floor. Any food items had disappeared a long time ago.

Papa and Jack stood deep in conversation, oblivious to her presence. "I can't change my stand on this, Mr. Garrison. I'm looking out for my daughter's best interests."

"Perhaps you don't know what is best for her." Jack crossed his arms.

They were talking about her and Jack. She put a hand over her mouth to stifle a gasp. What had Papa done?

She backed onto the sidewalk out front, stomped her feet, cleared her throat, and entered. The two men pulled apart and became instantly engrossed in inspecting the walls. She shook her head. A woman would have the problem solved by now. Lucy intended to speak to her father at the first opportunity and put her foot down as to her parents thinking they still had the right to control her life.

A crack in the ceiling overhead drew her attention. "Has that always been here?"

"No." Jack's curt answer sliced to her heart. "That will need to be fixed, just as this wall does. I hope all of the buildings aren't like this, or coming home will be days ahead of us."

"If we work together," Papa said, "we'll have everyone home before you know it. Businesses can be fixed last. Daughter, did you bring a pencil and paper?"

"Yes." Lucy dug a small paper pad from her pocket and stated the store's name and what needed fixing. The men headed to the next building, the village's small post office. This time, Lucy stayed close on their heels. She wasn't going to allow them any more time to talk about her behind her back.

By lunchtime, Lucy's stomach growled loud enough to rival the pounding waves on the nearby beach. She wanted to ask the men to take a break, but refused to show weakness of any kind. Instead, she guzzled water from the canteen slung over her shoulder, and continued to follow as the group went house to house.

She did manage to point out small things the men missed, such as dripping water in a roof corner, and cracks in foundations, but all in all, the homes seemed to be in pretty good condition, considering the back-to-back quakes that accompanied the volcano's eruption.

"Daughter, hand me a sandwich, would you?" Papa wiped a stained handkerchief across his brow. "I could use a break."

Thank you, God. Lucy handed out the meager lunch, taking hers to a bench that had somehow remained upright despite the surrounding damage of the sidewalk.

Her eyes, as hungry for any glimpse of Jack as her stomach was for the ham sandwich, followed as he plopped on an overturned barrel and ate, his gaze unfocused as he stared toward the sea. What was going on in that handsome head of his? If Papa had refused to give his blessing to allow Jack to court her, would he do so anyway? She doubted it. Jack was too much of a gentleman, despite what her parents thought.

Which meant, she needed to set her pursuits somewhere else. Not in a romantic sense, she didn't think she could find anyone that could hold a candle to Jack, but rather in a means of supporting herself as an adult and letting her parents know that, while she loved them, she was a self-sufficient adult. She smiled. She knew just the thing. Once they moved back into their cottage, she would set her plan in place.

~

Jack waded the greased paper his sandwich was wrapped in and shoved it into his pocket, trying not to notice the way the sun lit Lucy's hair with shots of blue, or how her cheeks darkened under the sun's heat. He failed miserably.

Despite her father's insistence that Jack keep his distance from his daughter, he intended to keep trying, and asking, until he got the answer he desired. No longer was he resolved to live the bachelor life. He'd got a taste of love again and meant to pursue the object of his affection. Until he won her father's blessing, he would do his best to keep his distance, but he would need God's help to do so.

In between asking for the blessing, Jack had dug for spiritual answers from Mr. Dillow and found his faith strengthening again. God hadn't killed his family, the sea had, and yet Jack stilled loved the ocean. How much more so should he still love God?

But, no amount of deep thought would provide relief from the heartache of loving Lucy. Not when her parents thought her out of Jack's league. Weren't all God's children the same? If Mr. Dillow had come to minister to the Hawaiian people, why was Jack, who once again chose to walk with God, still not good enough? Could it really be as simple as the Dillows fearing their daughter wouldn't be accepted?

Lucy joked and laughed with the other men who had accompanied them into town. Two of the men flirted shamelessly. Jack had been wrong at first, too, to think she wouldn't be accepted. His people loved her. Surely, in time, her parents would see it, too.

He stood and called for work to resume. Not only did they have the small street of businesses to inspect, but close to a hundred homes. It would take days to get through them all.

"Lucy, tack a sheet of paper with a check for those deemed safe enough for people to return to." He frowned at a group of tourists snapping photographs. When had shipping resumed? Before long, the nosy people would find their way to the refugee camp and disturb the peaceful semblance of life most had managed to gain for themselves.

"It's a pity," Mr. Dillow said, standing next to him. "The volcano, while dangerous and glorious, draws sightseers like bees to a flower. I wish the army had kept them away a bit longer."

Jack shrugged. "If we can keep them out of the damaged buildings, they should be fine. Obviously, we can scratch the Volcano House off our list. They wouldn't be receiving guests if the hotel was unsafe. Hopefully." He wanted to inform the tourists of the dangers, but decided to leave that to the army. It wasn't his place.

"Come along, Lucy," Mr. Dillow called. She stood staring into a small vacant building with a rent sign in the window. "We haven't checked that one yet."

"Let's check it now." She pushed open the door and stepped inside without waiting for the others.

Jack met her father's exasperated look, then hurried to join her. Nestled between two larger buildings, the tiny two story building still stood upright. No cracks marred the plaster walls or wooden floors. A tiny spiral staircase in the corner led to an upper loft.

"Everything in here looks fine," he said.

Lucy turned to him with a smile. "It's perfect." She jotted something in her notebook before closing it.

He thought it anything but perfect. The place was filled with dust and ash, the one window so dirty very little light managed to get in. He put out a hand to stop Lucy as she headed for the staircase. "I'll go first."

She nodded and stayed close on his heels as he climbed to the second floor. "A small kitchen!" She clapped her hands. "And a bed, a table, everything a person needs."

What was the woman up to now? Jack narrowed his eyes. She acted as if she were contemplating the place for herself. "Mark a check on the building and let's go."

With one more look over her shoulder, she headed down the stairs and joined the others outside. Her smile hadn't faded by the time Jack joined her, gaining him a frown from her father. Jack shrugged. If he was worried about Jack being alone in the building with Lucy, he should have followed them inside. There was too much work to be done for Jack to worry about imagined improprieties. If they didn't split up to examine the buildings, it would take longer than he had thought.

"We aren't going to make it to the homes today," Mr. Dillow stated. "But, with tourists arriving, it will be good to let the businesses back in."

Jack cut him a sideways glance. "You want to wait on the homes until the businesses are repaired?"

"We can have a majority vote at camp, but these people need to make a living. They have a place, although rustic, to lay their head right now."

"I need to head back anyway," Jack said. "Anake and the workers can return to my ranch. I'm needed to help herd the cattle."

"Then we will resume our efforts here tomorrow. I'll see about getting some volunteers to start repairing the buildings we've looked at, and another group to check what's left." He offered his hand. "We make a good team, Mr. Garrison."

Jack stared at his hand. Was he serious? A good team to work, but not for Lucy? He reluctantly returned the handshake and marched away, more confused than ever. How would the prejudiced missionaries react in a few weeks when Jack hired Filipino workers from the island of Kaui to help round up the cattle roaming the mountainside?

He laughed at the ludicrousness of it all. Even those who followed God as their mission in life needed work of the heart.

Back at the cottage he shared with Anake, he tossed his hat toward a hook on the wall, missed, left it there and plopped into a kitchen chair. Life was a lot less complicated before he met Lucy.

"Is your heart still troubled over the girl?" Anake set a slice of pineapple cake in front of him.

"Yes, and I don't want to talk about it." He picked up his fork and dug into his favorite dessert. "We're heading back to the ranch as soon as you can pack."

"I'm packed. Finished yesterday when you mentioned what you would be doing today. Your father built the ranch as solid as the mountain. I never feared harm would come to it."

He snorted. "Would have been a different story if the lava would have flowed that way, instead of into the sea."

She frowned. "Eat so we can move. Maybe your temperament will improve once you're home." She moved to the small sink and washed the cake dishes before stacking them into a box.

Jack carried his plate to the sink and planted a kiss on her round cheek. "I'm sorry."

She cupped his face. "Make a plan, Jack. If God wills it, Lucy Dillow will be yours."

That's what he was afraid of. What if it wasn't

God's plan for him and Lucy to marry? "You're a wise woman, Anake. I have a plan to win the heart of her parents in order to win Lucy's hand."

"Then don't fret. You can't change what won't be."

Actually, he probably could, but it wouldn't be wise. He'd get his home back in order and make himself indispensable to the Dillows.

10

With her heart in her throat, Lucy approached her parents after dinner. Papa glanced up from where he sat on a three-legged stool and smiled. What she had to say was going to break their hearts.

"Papa, Mama," she sat at their feet. "I'm nineteen years old and no longer desire to be under your rigid supervision. I've decided to rent a storefront and apartment in the village and sell my drawings to tourists."

"Absolutely not." Mama clutched her neckline. "A woman alone? It's preposterous."

Papa shook his head. "Daughter, I would lose sleep at night worrying about you. What if your drawings don't sell? What then?"

"I'd like to think that if my attempt at independence fails, you both would welcome me home."

Mama started to protest until Papa raised a hand to silence her. "Is this about Mr. Garrison?"

Lucy took a deep breath. "Partially. I overheard you and him talking in town this morning. While that opportunity may be out of my reach now, it did open my eyes to the fact that I very much desire to be independent and make my own decisions. At least I would like to try."

"You have no furniture," Mama said.

"The place is fully furnished and the rent is cheap." Lucy plucked at her skirt. "I truly believe, with the influx of tourists arriving on the island, that my drawings will sell. Especially the volcano ones. I'd like to also try my hand at color sketches."

Again, Mama tried to speak, only to have Papa stop her. "I am in agreement to let you try. If you fail and come home, you must then agree that your mother and I know what is best for you."

"Agreed." Lucy jumped up and threw her arms around his neck, glancing at her mother. "I hope you will want to sell some of your clothing designs in the shop, Mama."

"Foolishness." Still, a small smile tugged at her lips.

Lucy placed a kiss on her mother's forehead. "I'm going to gather my things. I want to move first thing in the morning."

"Come, my little flyaway birdie." Papa patted the stool next to him. "Enjoy one last cup of coffee with us before you go."

"Oh, Papa, there will be many coffees to be shared." Still, Lucy sat and poured herself a mug full. "I don't intend to stay away, you know. I'll have a lot of questions about how to make moving out successful."

"Our hut isn't too far from the shops. We'll be keeping a watchful eye on you," he said.

She didn't doubt it. Only moving off the island, which she didn't want to do, would guarantee true independence.

The next morning, her clothing and drawings in a handcart, Lucy headed down the business street of the village and into her new home. She'd located the owner before approaching her parents the day before and obtained the key. She had a lot of work to do, cleaning her new home, but wanted a sign in the window by morning advertising her drawings and the opportunity for tourists to have their portrait drawn.

Jack strolled down the opposite sidewalk and cast a questioning look her way. She tossed him a wave and unlocked her door. While small and dirty, she was home. She rolled the handcart inside and looked for a broom. Not finding one, she stepped back outside and approached Papa and Jack, who stood outside a building two doors down.

"Do either of you know where I can get a broom and a bucket?"

"I can't believe you let her move into a place alone." Jack shook his head at Papa.

"What I allow my daughter to do, is no concern of yours." Papa faced her. "There are some cleaning supplies in the shop next to you. Please replace them when you are finished."

"How will she make a living? Who will keep her safe?" Jack leaned against the building.

"I can manage those things on my own, thank you." Lucy marched away. How dare he interfere in her life? If he cared so much, he would defy her father's wishes and propose to her. Since he hadn't, she believed he hadn't cared as much as she had thought. They were never, nor would they ever be, anything more than friends.

She sniffed back tears and went in search of the supplies she needed to turn her space into a home. She would show them all just how much one determined woman could accomplish.

Tears and perspiration ran down her face as she swept ash from inside her shop to outside. She wiped her face on her sleeve and glanced toward the mountain. Lush greenery grew a few hundred feet toward the volcano before everything turned dark. To her right, a breeze blew the ash from the foliage, revealing the vibrant colors of the island. Life was returning to normal.

Except for hers. She was embarking a new adventure. An exciting new chapter in her life. A chapter she had desperately wanted to share with the handsome cowboy eating lunch across the street. She huffed. She hadn't thought to bring food with her to her new home. Just what did she intend to eat until she gained funds?

Papa came her way, a basket slung over his arm. "I'm sorry. Your mother sent this basket over and I've just now remembered it. It should feed you until I deliver another one in the morning."

"Oh, Papa, I was just thinking about food."

He laughed. "I could tell from the way you were devouring Mr. Garrison's sandwich with your eyes." His laughter stopped. "Or was it the man you were looking at so intently?"

"Stop." She took the basket. "Thank you for the food, but my life is now my own. You've managed to run Mr. Garrison off and set me on the path to spinsterhood. I fear you have no worries in that area." She lifted the lid on the basket. "Oh, wherever did Mama get the rice rolls?" She really needed to learn the proper names of Hawaiian food.

"One of the women she helped this morning." Papa hugged her. "Good luck, but don't expect this old man to stop worrying about his only child. It is impossible."

"I love you, Papa. Thank mother for the food." Lucy couldn't get inside fast enough.

She carried the basket upstairs and quickly set the few dishes and food items on her one and only shelf before perching on the side of her bed to devour one of the sweet rice rolls. Once she had eaten, she had the strength to continue cleaning. She also wanted to go through her sketches to choose the ones to sell, and the ones to send to Mr. Woodward. Those, she would resketch in order to have duplicates to sell. With her first earnings, she would purchase a box of colored pencils or chalk.

"Hello?"

She peered over the banister to the floor below. "Come in, Jack."

"I've brought you a small table and two chairs." He waved a hand and three men carried in the furniture. "Where would you like them?"

"Up here would be perfect." She quickly shoved her bed against the wall to make room.

Jack helped carry the scarred table. "Your father found this in a cottage that has been vacated. Its previous owner has relocated to Maui."

"It's perfect." She beamed up at him, her smile fading when he didn't return the gesture. She was going to invite him for a walk along the beach that evening, too. It was just as well. Her parents not only shut down what might have turned into a lasting relationship, but they seemed to have destroyed a friendship as well. She swallowed the mountain in her throat and fought to keep a smile on her face. "Thank you."

He nodded, a muscle ticking in his jaw, his eyes intent on her face, before he turned and clomped down the stairs. Lucy sagged into one of the rickety chairs. She gave herself a few seconds to mourn, then forced herself back to work. She still intended to take that walk later and enjoy the cool ocean breeze.

The sun had set farther than she had expected by the time she had her home to rights and was able to dig her bare toes into the moist sand. Unmindful of her skirt, she sat, wrapping her arms around her bent knees and listened to the pounding of the surf. She had released her hair from its bun and let the breeze tease the strands with a salty spray.

Eyes closed, she lifted her face and prayed for guidance.

~

Jack should not have expressed his displeasure to Mr. Dillow about Lucy spreading her wings. The man was right. It was none of Jack's business.

Still, as he gazed upon her sitting on the beach, his heart lay heavy. While work on the ranch ran smooth because of workers like Manuel, Jack still had things he needed to keep an eye on. Things that did not include a half hour horseback ride to keep an eye on Lucy, especially when the extra workers from Kaui arrived. They were a rough bunch of men. If they found out she was living alone—he couldn't stomach thinking about it.

Watching her unawares did no good for either of them. He turned and headed for his horse. It was going to be a long, lonely night.

He rode through the deepening darkness around the perimeter of the camp. Most folks had chosen to go home, doing the repairs while living in their building. Not something Jack advised, but they were entitled, unless the building was condemned by authorities greater than he. Still, a few tents blinked under the moonlight.

Muffled conversations drifted through the canvas walls as husbands and wives conversed and mothers soothed anxious children. He wanted things to return to normal as much as the next person. Only, his normal had changed. He couldn't lay his head on his pillow at night without falling asleep to Lucy's face flitting across his mind.

He frowned at the trampled pasture land. It was going to be a task feeding his cattle through the year. He tried to think of another place they could graze while his hired hands rounded up strays. Land was limited on an island and shipping them to another island was unheard of. He sighed and steered toward home.

Anake had left a light burning in the kitchen to welcome him back. He couldn't help but think how wonderful it would be if Lucy waited for him on the lanai. A man never knew how lonely he could be until he fell in love with a woman out of his reach. What was once sufficient in his life had become grossly insufficient.

Not wanting to disturb his stable-boy from his slumber, Jack brushed and cared for his horse before trudging to the house. He stopped a few feet from the door and studied the rambling ranch style home. His mother had designed the house and his father had built it. They had been a happy family once. Jack yearned to fill the rooms again.

An orange glow in the direction of town attracted his attention. It took a few seconds for it to register for what it was. Fire! Lucy.

He dashed back to the barn to resaddle his poor horse. Within fifteen minutes, he was racing for town. He passed Mr. and Mrs. Dillow, clothed in nightgowns and robes, also rushing toward the fire. He stopped long enough for Lucy's mother to climb behind them, then hurried on, leaving Mr. Dillow to follow.

"I knew we shouldn't have left her on her own," Mrs. Dillow wailed in his ear.

"We don't know that Lucy is in any danger." A fist gripped his heart and squeezed.

He stopped in front of the post office. Across the street, flames shot through the roof of a café. He'd warned the owners not to try and resume business until the building was prepared. This is what happened when people didn't listen.

He helped Mrs. Dillow to the ground, then slid from the saddle. Lucy ran toward them. Her mother grabbed her in a fierce hug.

"I'm fine, Mama." She turned to stare at the flames. "Those poor people."

"Did they get out?" Jack looped the reins over a post.

"Yes." Tear tracks marred her face. "I've been going door-to-door alerting residents and hunting for blankets."

"Tell me you haven't been fighting the fire." Mrs. Dillow put a shaky hand over her mouth.

"Of course, I have." Lucy frowned. "And, I need to get back to it. Jack?"

"Right behind you." He placed a hand on Mrs. Dillow's shoulder. "I'll watch out for her."

She nodded, her face grim. "I know you will." She sagged on a bench. "I'll wait here for my husband. He will want us to minister to the owners."

"That is something you could do while waiting for him." Jack motioned his head toward the owners, the wife sobbing in her husband's arms.

"You think so?" She picked at the lace on the cuff of her robe. "Will they accept me?"

"Of course, they will. We aren't as hard headed as you think we are." He stomped away, heading for a well at the edge of town where a bucket brigade was in full force.

Did she think so little of the people she had come to help that she was afraid to even pray for them without her husband? He had a harder battle convincing her to let him court Lucy than he had thought. The poor woman seemed terrified of practically everything.

He spotted Anake bustling in his direction. He stopped her. "Could you please go with Mrs. Dillow to pray with the Daneses? She seems a bit … shy."

"Of course." She gripped his arm. "I've just received news that my sister is ill. I'm leaving for

Maui in a few minutes, but I have time for a prayer."

"I'll miss you." He kissed her cheek. "I hope your sister will be fine. I've got to go."

She nodded and joined Lucy's mother. Together they approached the owners of the café.

Jack grabbed two full buckets, although he could tell at first glance the building was unsalvageable. In hopes to save the fabric store next door, he tossed water on the wood shingled roof.

Lucy hurried to his side, buckets in hand, her hem wet and muddy around her bare feet. "We're fighting a losing battle."

"Tell the others to focus on the buildings on each side. This one can't be saved." He tossed the water, and then followed her back to the well. He went one way to tell others of his plan, while Lucy headed in the other. By now, Mr. Dillow had joined them.

"What a tragedy on top of everything else that has befallen this island." He soaked a blanket.

"The islanders are tough. They'll survive." Some might give up and move to another island, but most would dig their feet in and stay.

Lucy, her hands empty of buckets, but hitching her skirt to her knees, raced past them. Jack turned as a kitten darted into the shop to the west of the burning building. Lucy ducked a sagging timber and disappeared.

Jack dropped his bucket and rushed after her. What was the silly woman thinking? Already, blowing embers had set the roof on fire. The entire structure could collapse on top of her.

"Lucy!" He shoved aside a curtain starting to burn and covered his nose and mouth with his shirt collar. Smoke filled the room. "Where are you?"

"Here!"

He followed her voice to the back of the building. Grabbing her around the waist, he pulled her from under a table. "Are you crazy!?"

"There's kitten. Oh, Jack, the poor thing is so scared." She yanked free and fell to her knees."

"No, Lucy. Not even a kitten is worth your life." Smoke stung his eyes. He squatted next to her. "We have to leave."

"Got it!" She crawled backward, the kitten shoved into her robe, its wide eyes peering over the top button.

The roof groaned over their heads. Jack grabbed her arm and pulled her toward the door. She would be the death of him. He coughed as tears streamed down his face. Lucy didn't seem to be faring much better.

She covered her mouth and shrank against him as a roof beam fell. The hem of her gown caught on fire. She screamed, the sound cut off by fierce coughing. "I'm ... so ... sorry."

"Apologize later." He shoved her toward the door.

The building shuddered. He gave Lucy a mighty push and covered his head as the roof collapsed. The last thing he heard was her calling his name.

11

"Jack!" Lucy tugged at a smoldering beam. Her hands burned before she thought to wrap them in her robe. "Somebody help us!"

"I'm here." Manuel pushed her to the side. Grabbing the beam, he hefted it to one side and dragged an unconscious Jack from the fire.

Lucy whipped off what was left of her robe and slapped at the flames on his legs. *Please, open your eyes, Jack. Please.* "I can't live without you," she whispered, her throat raw from smoke.

"Let me help." Papa took over, quickly extinguishing the parts of his clothing that smoldered. "Do we have a doctor in town?"

Manuel shook his head. "Anake was the best we had. She is gone for now."

Lucy's heart sank. "I'll care for him. We must get him to his ranch."

"No." Mama swung her around. "Think of your reputation."

"Then come with me." Lucy gripped her mother's shoulders. "You have more nursing experience than I do. Please. He saved my life."

Her mother took a deep breath, coughed, and took charge. "Load him in that wagon. We must get him out of the burned clothing as soon as possible." She clapped her hands, spurring the others into action.

Two other men rushed to help and soon had Jack in the back of the wagon. Manuel started to climb into the driver's seat.

"No." Mama stopped him. "I know how to drive a wagon. You're needed to help stop the fire from spreading. Papa, head to the base. Surely, they have a military doctor there." As if her words had conjured them, a jeep of soldiers stopped in front of them, filling the air with dust.

"We're here to help." The driver, the same man who had stopped Lucy a few days before, leaped to the ground. "We have a medic that will go with you to Mr. Garrison's ranch." With a few hand gestures, he sent the soldiers scattering.

Lucy didn't wait for help. She didn't care about propriety. Hiking her gown to her knees, she climbed into the wagon beside Jack. His once long hair had been burnt to around his ears. Even in the moonlight, she could see the redness of the burns on his neck. She wanted to take him in her arms and never let go. She would have, if not for fear of causing him more pain.

"He's in good hands, miss." The army medic, Sergeant Miller, sliced through Jack's shirt with a knife, peeling the fabric from his body. "I'll give him a shot of morphine. I can't accurately assess the damage until I have some light."

Mama flicked the reins and sent the wagon bouncing toward the ranch. Sergeant Miller frowned and folded Jack's shirt under his head, muttering something about the rough road doing more damage than the fire.

Lucy doubted it. She wiped her streaming eyes on the sleeve of her gown and shoved her hair out of her face. Jack wouldn't recognize her when he opened his eyes, she was so covered in dirt and soot. Thankfully, the thick cotton nightdress was as modest as her day clothes and kept her from being embarrassed by a strange man sitting across from her. She scooted against the wall of the wagon bed, her eyes never leaving Jack's face as if her gaze would keep him breathing.

Wrapping her arms around her bent knees, she prayed, her eyes still open, for Jack's recovery. "He shoved me out of the way," she said.

"From what I've heard of Mr. Garrison, he's that kind of man." Sergeant Miller scooted against the far wall. "What's your name?"

"Lucy Dillow. The wild driver of the wagon is my mother."

"Let me see your hands." He held out one of his.

Lucy bent forward, showing him her burns. It wasn't until she caught a glimpse of her red palms that she realized how bad the burns were.

"I'll need to tend to you, too, once we have Mr. Garrison taken care of." Miller shook his head. "Try not to use them until I can get them cleaned and bandaged."

"You're hurt?" Mama darted a look over her shoulder. "Why didn't you tell me?"

"Jack needs the attention more."

"Sergeant, I will tend to my daughter while you

care for Mr. Garrison."

He shot Lucy an amused glance. "Yes, ma'am."

Lucy turned her attention back to Jack. Clouds covered the moon. She scooted closer and put her cheek next to his mouth to determine whether he still breathed.

He pressed his lips to her skin. "I'm here."

A sob ripped from her throat. "You frightened me. Don't ever do that again, Jack. Garrison."

"I can promise you that if you are in danger, I will ... put myself in danger's path ... every time."

"Oh, Jack." With the tip of her finger, she smoothed his bangs from his eyes.

The wagon jostled over a crack in the road. He groaned and closed his eyes, drifting again into slumber.

"Careful, Mama." Lucy tapped her shoulder.

"I'm doing my best. The road is atrocious. Someone should really make repairing it a priority."

"The people are busy repairing their lives." Lucy bit back any further retorts. Mama, not used to such tragedy was doing her best, and surprisingly, Lucy was doing the same. If someone would have told her yesterday that her mother would fight a fire, then drive a wagon like a mad woman, she would have told them they were crazy.

Mama pulled the wagon as close to the ranch house as possible, then slid to the ground. "I'm not sure the three of us can get a man his size into the house."

"I can walk ... with help." Jack pushed up on his elbows. "Don't worry about the bed, just get me to the sofa. And I think someone mentioned morphine?"

The sergeant chuckled. "As soon as you're settled. I didn't want to risk a shot in a bouncing wagon." He jumped to the ground.

As Jack joined him, the man put his arm around Jack's waist and Jack's arm over his shoulder. "Miss Dillow, if you could get the other side, please?"

Lucy rushed to help. Together, they managed to get Jack up the two steps to the lanai and into the house. Mama hurried to prop up the sofa pillows on one end for Jack to rest his head. "I'll get some fresh water in a pot and be right back."

Jack sucked air through his teeth as he was lowered to the sofa. It physically hurt Lucy to see him in so much pain. She rubbed her itching palms on her thighs, only to hiss and jerk them back.

"Come into the kitchen, Lucy," Mama called. "Let the sergeant get Jack into clean clothes."

Speaking of clothes ... Lucy needed something herself. She grinned at the thought of wearing one of Anake's muumuus. Mama must have had the same thought. She stood at the sink dressed in a bright green one with yellow flowers. Across one of the chairs was spread a purple one with pink flowers.

"We won't be exactly stylish." Mama grinned. "But these are clean and comfortable. I don't think I've felt this free in a dress since I was a young girl. Take a sponge bath, then let me see those hands. This is a lovely home."

Lucy glanced around the sprawling kitchen.

Cabinets filled one wall with a breakfast island in the center for extra preparation space. Cheery yellow curtains fluttered from a window, giving a far off view of the sea. She hadn't paid a lot of attention as they had carried Jack inside, but she had noticed that the living area was filled with ornate wood pieces and leather furniture.

"Yes. It's beautiful." She plunged her hand into the pot. Even lukewarm water stung her hands, but Lucy pushed through and cleaned the best she could before donning the dress that fit her like a tent. She started to rush back to the living room, when her mother stopped her.

"No, you don't. Sit and let me bandage those hands." She pointed to a chair. "Besides, you don't want to barge in and find Mr. Garrison … indecent."

Lucy plopped into a chair, her face flaming as much as her hands. She wanted to slink through the floorboards. Mama probably already thought propriety flew out the window when Lucy helped a bare-chested Jack into the house. She hadn't thought anything of it at the time, but now her mind drifted in a completely improper direction.

She actually welcomed the pain of Mama's ministrations, as it returned her thoughts back where they belonged.

~

"How bad is it?" Jack opened his eyes and stared into the face of a stranger. "Because it feels bad." A needle pricked his arm.

"You'll need to regrow your hair." The sergeant grinned. "The ladies cut it pretty short to get rid of the scorched parts. You've also got burns on your hands, neck, and shoulders. The worst ones are on your legs, but you'll be fine. Some scarring on the legs, considering your pants caught fire, but the others will fade."

"Like the room is fading?"

"That, Mr. Hero, is the morphine." The sergeant covered him with a thin blanket. "I'll drive the buggy back to town and leave you in the capable hands of the lovely Miss Dillow and her mother. I'll be back in the morning to check on you."

"Mrs. Dillow is here?" Egads! Did he really say that? "The woman hates me."

"I do not hate you, Mr. Garrison." Mrs. Dillow glared. "If you're speaking to the good sergeant, he left ten minutes ago. I simply don't think you suitable material for my daughter, and I don't mean that as anything against you being half-native. I only believe that she doesn't know what is best for her. The island is not it."

Why did his tongue feel so thick? "No offense."

"You aren't making any sense, Mr. Garrison. I will chalk your earlier comment up to the medicine. Now, sit up and let me feed you some broth."

"Lucy."

"She is sleeping."

He frowned. "Is she okay?"

"Burns on her hands from trying to pull you from the building, but she will be fine. I slipped some powder I found in the cabinet in her drink. She'll see you in a few hours."

"You should sleep."

"I will in a moment. Now, open your mouth."

He obeyed, feeling like a child who had gotten into his father's brandy. While the pain in his body had subsided, he disliked the fuzzy feeling in his head or the inability to filter his thoughts before they escaped his lips. "I love your daughter."

"Everyone loves Lucy."

He narrowed his eyes. "You know what I mean."

"Unfortunately, I do." She gave a sad smile and sighed. "A few more bites before you fall asleep."

The next time he awoke, Lucy sat in the chair beside the sofa, her sketchbook open on her lap. She held a pencil in her fingers, her hands bandaged, but her gaze rested on him instead of her drawing.

"Good afternoon," she said.

"I slept that long?" He struggled to a sitting position, the burned skin on his legs pulling.

"Sergeant Miller has come and gone, saying you seem to be doing fine, with no infection. Would you like some morphine?"

"No. That stuff is atrocious. Does funny things to a man."

She plumped the pillows behind him. "Let me fetch you some tea."

"You look adorable in that muumuu."

She giggled, her cheeks turning pink. "Ridiculous is more like it, but I love wearing it."

"I'm sorry you were injured trying to help me."

She tilted her head. "You saved my life, Jack. I owe you everything. A bit of skin is nothing in comparison. I'll be right back."

While she was only gone for only minutes, it

seemed much longer. She returned the same time her mother entered through the front door.

"Your workers are back and taking care of your stock," Mrs. Dillow said, shaking out her apron. "I couldn't find the chickens. Why don't you have a coop?"

"My housekeeper knows where they hide. Don't worry about the eggs." Jack grimaced and flung the blanket off his legs. The day was warming up too hot for such a covering.

"You aren't supposed to be moving around." Lucy set the tea on the side table. "Don't make Mama have to tie you down."

"You're in the same boat, missy." Mrs. Dillow planted fists on her hips. "What possessed you to pour tea with bandaged hands? Are you asking for another disaster?"

"Jack wanted tea."

Jack shook his head when the woman turned her glare on him. "She offered. I'm not thinking clearly." How was he going to survive these two? He understood why Lucy couldn't stay alone with him, but that didn't keep him from wishing it. They could talk of the future … Oh. He remembered they didn't have a future, and returned Mrs. Dillow's glare.

"I'm tired." He lay back down and turned his head to face the back of the sofa. Though he appreciated the woman's help, really, but he was tired of being reminded how unsuited he was for Lucy. If saving her life didn't raise his esteem in Mrs. Dillow's eyes, what would?

He closed his eyes and listened as Lucy's

pencil scratched across her pad. What could she find in the house to sketch? While he loved the sprawling home, it wasn't something an artist's eye would be drawn to, was it? His eyes closed the pleasant sound of Mrs. Dillow humming as she cleaned.

When he woke again, the sun was setting outside. He was going to miss his nightly routine of drinking coffee on the lanai. "Lucy, help me outside."

"Not until you put on a shirt." Mrs. Dillow flapped a white cotton shirt at him. "Then, we'll both join you on the lanai. I've coffee on the stove."

"You're a marvel, Mrs. Dillow. It's as if you can read my mind." He slipped his good arm through the sleeve and let her drape the other over his shoulder, pinning it together in the front. She sure went to a lot of trouble to make sure Lucy didn't see his chest.

"I know more than you think I do." She glanced from him to her daughter.

"Mama." Lucy rolled her eyes. "Ignore her, Jack." She slipped her shoulder under his arm. "Catch him if he falls, Mama."

They made their way to the lanai, Mrs. Dillow getting him and Lucy situated before heading back inside. Jack watched her leave, then turned to Lucy. "I think I'm growing on her."

She laughed. "Don't mind Mama. She's a bit opinionated, but I'm learning there is a lot more to her than I originally thought."

"She's a good woman." Jack caressed her cheek. "She has your best interests at heart."

She turned sparkling hazel eyes to him. "Not exactly."

He lowered his head to try and steal a kiss, but jerked back when Mrs. Dillow returned with a silver tray bearing tiny sandwiches and a carafe of coffee. He stared at the food. "What are these? They hardly make a mouthful."

"They're finger sandwiches, Mr. Garrison." She set the tray on a small table. "You really need to learn a bit of culture."

"I know all about my culture that I need to." He popped a piece in his mouth, savoring the taste of ham and pineapple spread. "Delicious. What's the green one?"

"Cucumber." She poured him a cup of coffee. "You two eat, and I'll be back in a few minutes. I've just discovered you have an indoor bathtub. I thought only the hotel did."

"A few minutes of peace." Lucy grinned up at him. "I think you were going to kiss me."

"Do you want me to?"

"If you aren't too injured."

"That sounds like a challenge." With his finger, he tilted her face to his and laid his lips on hers. She was as soft as he remembered, the kiss as sweet. To think he almost lost her the day before tore at his gut. He tightened his hold on her, only to straighten at the sound of her mother's footsteps approaching.

"Hot water, too!" Mrs. Dillow exclaimed through the open door. "If you don't need anything right now, I'm going to soak."

Lucy waved her hand. "Don't worry about us."

"Hmm. Behave."

"She's so excited about indoor plumbing," Jack said. "She isn't thinking of all the trouble we can get into out here alone."

"Oh, stop." Lucy giggled. "Other than kisses, there isn't much we can do. You are in no shape to even take a walk on the beach." She ducked her head. "I've missed those."

"Your father was very clear in his wanting me to stay away from you."

"Speaking of …" She motioned her head toward the walk leading to the house. "It looks as if you have the entire Dillow family under your roof."

Jack stiffened, fully expecting an attack from Mr. Dillow. Instead, the man shook his hand, thanked him for saving Lucy, then asked where his wife was.

"She's taking a bath," Lucy said.

"Inside?" Mr. Dillow lunged for the door. "It's been a long time." The door slammed shut behind him.

Jack laughed, the movement paining his shoulders. Still, he couldn't quit. "It seems as if a hot bath is more important than your reputation at the moment."

"Then I suggest you make the most of the opportunity and give me a kiss."

12

Lucy stepped out of the tub and dressed in a simple navy skirt and white blouse. Every morning of the week she had been in Jack's home, she had taken a bath. The luxury was worth the stinging of her still tender palms. Thankfully, the bandages were gone and she no longer needed her mother's help to bathe and dress.

She could get used to such luxury, and from Mama's constant humming as she worked around the house, she'd guess her mother felt the same. Could that be Mama's problem? Was it as simple as her missing modern luxuries? If so, then the fire was a mixed blessing in the Ellis family. Slowly, but surely, Mama was warming to Jack. In fact, Lucy had heard her laughing with him while fixing breakfast the morning before.

After putting her hair in a bun, she grabbed a basket from a hook on the kitchen wall, glanced to where Jack snored from the sofa, and headed outside. She would find out where Anake's chickens hid if it took her all day. Jack told her not to worry about it, they could always purchase some in town, but why throw away money when eggs were lying on your land?

She strolled toward a batch of beach grass. There they were. Three little beauties. She gently placed the eggs in the basket and continued to search the area, coming up with a few more that seagulls hadn't found. After a week of lounging, she needed something to occupy her time, and menial chores seemed the best route. She wanted to begin school again soon, too, since most of the families seemed to have settled back into their homes.

"Good morning." Jack stepped to her side. "You're quite the treasure seeker."

She turned to him with a smile. "I thought like a chicken."

He laughed. "And how does a chicken think, exactly?"

"Well," she cocked her head, "they want a place that is relatively safe, such as thick grass, and in a place that is off the beaten path. I must confess that I headed to this rise in order to watch the waves and got lucky."

"Your father told me that you'll be returning home soon."

Lucy's heart fell. "But you're still wearing bandages. Your shoulder is stiff." She sighed. "Mama will be heartbroken to leave this place."

"Only your mother? What about the daughter?" He turned her to face him, his dark eyes fixed on her face.

"I don't want to leave either." Her face heated.

"Lucy!" Mama called from the house.

"Come on." Lucy glanced at the house. "It's time for the medic, and you shouldn't be wandering around. What if you fell?"

"I'm healing nicely. There is no longer a need for me to be treated like a child, but I'll pretend if it will keep you here longer." He gave her a quick one-armed hug and stepped away as they neared the house.

Lucy handed the basket of eggs to her mother and brushed past her into the living room to greet the arriving Sergeant Miller. "Come in. Your patient insists on walking around."

"He's able to. Movement is the best thing for him. The burns, thank God, weren't life threatening. Come, Mr. Garrison. Let me take a look."

Lucy grabbed her sketch pad and headed to the lanai. If Papa had his way, this would be their last day on the ranch. She wanted to capture as many of the images as she could. She giggled thinking of Mama's reaction if Lucy should draw the tub with Mama in it. Of course, she would only draw the back of her head, but the indoor plumbing would be what Mama missed the most.

The low murmuring of Jack and the sergeant drifted through the open window. An ocean breeze ruffled the curtains. Lucy would definitely miss waking up each morning to the sound of Jack's deep voice and the sight of his handsome face.

"Lucy?" Mama stepped around the corner of the house. "Come walk with me. Let's take one more meander around this beautiful place."

She set her sketch pad on the rocker and hurried to meet her mother. Tears stung the back of her eyes. She was sure her expression matched the sad one of Mama.

Mama took a deep breath. "I do love the scent of plumeria blossoms."

"Maybe we can plant some outside of our hut." Lucy linked her arm through her mother's and led the way to the same rise she had stood on earlier with Jack. "I wish we could stay."

"We cannot." Mama stopped and gazed at the ocean. "But, I have come to see why you love this island."

"And the people."

Mama nodded. "One person in particular. Oh, Lucy, don't you see the hardship that might be yours if you stay with him?"

"Might being the important word here." Lucy dug her feet into the sand. "I'm willing to take my chances. Why won't you and Papa let me find some things out for myself?"

"We want to spare you heartache." Mama twisted her hands in her skirt. "Have I ever told you the story of when I met your father?"

"You said you met him at church."

"That is true, but I never expanded on our courtship. Let's sit." Mama spread her skirts and sat on a clump of grass. "I was raised with wealth. Even more than Mr. Garrison most likely has. Your father was a poor theological student. Needless to say, my parents did not approve. We eloped, against their wishes. While I love your father very much, and have never regretted marrying him, our life has not been an easy one." She shifted to look at Lucy. "If you were to marry Mr. Garrison, your life could be harder than the one I chose. As your mother, I wish to spare you that."

"So, you would rather ship me to the mainland and have me marry someone I don't love?" Lucy plucked at a strand of grass. "Besides, Mr. Garrison hasn't asked me to marry him. While we are attracted to each other, something stills his hand." She choked on her words. "What if he is only toying with me?"

"You don't believe that." Mama patted her hand. "The sun sets and rises on you as far as that man is concerned. I think he is waiting to win over your father before declaring himself."

"Has he won you over?" Hope rushed through Lucy with the force of a volcano's eruption.

"It's hard not to admire the man, especially after seeing what he has accomplished on this island. Do you know he plans on building a church and a school?" Awe laced her words.

"He's made mention of it." Would Mama speak with Papa if Lucy asked? Had she changed enough to believe that love can conquer all?

Mama expelled a deep breath. "I know you are going to do what you want. I can only ask that you spend a lot of time in prayer before making your decision."

"You won't force me to go with you when you leave here?"

"No. You are old enough to form your own future." Mama wrapped her arms around her. "But, I will miss you so very much."

The tears Lucy had held back burst free and slid down her cheeks. "I love you. Thank you for understanding, if not for giving your blessing."

"I do like the man, dear, and I am growing

quite fond of these hard-working, fun-loving people. I can see why you are so enamored." She kissed the top of Lucy's head. "Let's head back so I can cook lunch. I only have a few meals left to cook on that wonderful stove."

If Jack ever proposed to Lucy, she would insist her parents move onto the ranch with them. They could build a smaller home on the land and never leave the island. Why, Papa could preach at the new church! Life would be grand.

She pushed to her feet and strolled back to the house with her mother. Mama entered through the back kitchen door, leaving Lucy to head around front to collect her pad and pencil. She turned the corner and stopped. Papa sat in the rocker, flipping through her sketches, his face grim.

Slapping the pad closed, he stormed into the house, the slamming of the door like the tolling of a bell in the final hour.

~

"Mr. Garrison, I don't think you took our conversation about Lucy to heart." Mr. Dillow tossed Lucy's sketch pad onto Jack's lap.

Jack set down the newspaper he was reading. "I have no idea what you're talking about. Other than my helping her gather eggs this morning, we haven't been alone." He left out the times Mrs. Dillow took her evening bath, leaving the two of them alone on the lanai. "I promise you, I have not been courting your daughter."

"This tells a different story." He tapped the pad with his forefinger.

Jack raised his brows and flipped open the pad.

Interspersed with drawings of the island were detailed portraits of him in various poses and doing different jobs. His heart swelled. Regardless of her parents' wishes, Lucy cared enough about him to make sure she had something lasting to take with her when she left. He grinned.

"I'll thank you to wipe the smile off your face, Mr. Garrison." Mr. Dillow groaned and plopped into a chair. "Who am I kidding? You and my daughter are going to defy mine and my wife's wishes and court behind our backs."

Jack remained silent, guilt filling him at the man's words. If his own mother were alive, or Anake here to witness the exchange, they would be very disappointed in the fact that Jack clearly defied the wishes of Mr. Dillow.

"Sir, I think it's best we change the subject." Jack placed the sketchbook on the table, planning to look at it again. "I am planning on building a schoolhouse and a church, and sincerely want your input on both. I understand your feelings about Lucy and I, but am asking that you agree to work by my side and live under my roof while we accomplish this together."

"My wife would like that, for sure." He rubbed his chin. "I'm not sure about you and my daughter remaining in such close proximity together."

"I will be busy at the work site and overseeing the Filipino workers that should arrive sometime tomorrow. If it makes you feel any better, I'll have little chance of saying one word to Lucy" He thought it best to leave out that the longer Mr. Dillow was around Jack, the more certain he was to approve of a courtship. At least, that was Jack's plan.

"Hmm. You are up to something, Mr. Garrison. I'm not a fool. I know exactly what is going through that mind of yours, but I am not one to turn down something that will help the majority." He thrust out his hand. "Partners?"

Jack returned the shake. "Partners." He pulled a stack of papers from under a book and slid them to Mr. Dillow. "In the nights when my injuries kept me from sleeping well, I drew up some plans. I'd value your input."

Mr. Dillow peered at Jack's neck. "Very little scarring. You are a lucky man. God must have plans for you, considering you came close to dying."

Plans like marrying Lucy? "My legs fared worse, but I'm not a vain man." Except for his hair. Anake always said he was as bad as a woman in regards to his shiny mane. Unfortunately, Mrs Dillow had cut his hair above where it had scorched, leaving him looking like a foreigner.

"These are very good." Mr. Dillow straightened. "My only suggestion is that you could possibly build a parsonage, instead of a school, and use this room you have allocated as a Sunday school room for school, until you have the means to build another building. A parsonage would go a long way toward enticing a preacher to the island."

"I was hoping you would take the position, sir."

"Thus, keeping Lucy close."

Jack grinned. "That had crossed my mind."

The flicker of a smile tugged at Mr. Dillow's

mouth. "You are a persistent man. Let me spend some time in prayer and discuss the matter with my wife."

"I'll make sure the parsonage has indoor plumbing." Jack's grin spread. "Make sure and tell Mrs. Dillow."

"You are a sneaky man." He threw back his head and laughed. "She won't be able to resist the tub. That might be hard to find on the mainland as a traveling missionary." He sobered. "But, you're asking for a life change. I can't give you my answer right away."

"I understand." Jack replaced the building plans into a neat pile and slid them back under the heavy book he used to keep them in place. "But, I believe you might reach more of the islanders if you have a building to preach in. Even the tourists may attend your services."

"Food for thought, my good man." He slapped his hands on his thighs and pushed to his feet. "I will let you know my decision in good time. In the meantime," he smiled, "get started building." He headed outside, holding the door open for Lucy.

Jack handed her the sketch pad and winked. "I had an interesting conversation with your father."

She blushed. "I'm sure you did." She grabbed the pad, clutched it to her chest, and dashed from the room as if her skirts were on fire.

He'd had no idea she drew so many likenesses of him. Her feelings for him must run deep, and while he was willing to wait for her parents' blessing, he felt that she might say yes if he proposed at that moment.

He stood and moved to the window. He wanted to, very much, but what kind of life would they have if her parents disagreed? Lucy and her mother may clash at times, but he knew they loved each other fiercely. It would break Lucy's heart if her parents turned their back on her. He could not be the cause of that.

Squinting, he made out the shape of Anake bustling up the walk. He rushed to greet her, sweeping her into his arms for a hug. "I've missed you."

"Sure you have." She slapped his shoulder, thankfully, the good one. "You've already put another woman in my kitchen, if the stories I've heard are correct. Let me look at you." She stepped back and cocked her head. "I've been worried after hearing a roof collapsed on you. I should have been here to care for you. You're my boy."

He drew her close again. "I've been well cared for. How is your sister?"

"Fine. Nothing but gout." She sighed. "So, your lady is here?"

"And her parents." Jack released her. "It's been an interesting week."

"I suppose it has." She rubbed her hands together. "The workers will be arriving tomorrow. I'd better go see whether Mrs. Dillow is willing to help me keep them fed."

Another reason for the Dillow family to remain under his roof. The day kept getting better and better. Not only would he have more time with Lucy and her family, but the much needed rounding up of his cattle was getting close. After the volcanic eruption, time had almost seemed to stand still as far as his work went. He rotated his burned shoulder. Other than some tenderness and pulling, he was ready to dive back into work.

With a spring in his step, he headed for the bunkhouse to go over the workload with Manuel. With them expecting up to ten strangers in the morning, he needed to make sure they had room to sleep and that rules were posted.

"It's not looking good, boss." Manuel met him in the yard. "Rumors of an uprising on the island of Kaui are reaching us here. The Filipinos are angry at the foreign landowners."

"We should be fine, then." Jack continued toward the bunkhouse. "I'm a native."

"But you live like a haole."

"The drovers may work ten to twelve hours a day, but I pay them a fair wage." Jack shook his head. "You worry too much over rumors."

"You don't worry enough." Manuel tapped his chest. "You are thinking with your heart and not your head. Look around you. You live like a king and have brought foreigners under your roof. These workers may not be happy."

Jack's blood chilled. Was he exposing Lucy and her parents to danger in his selfish desire to keep Lucy close?

13

"I'm going to town," Lucy told Jack and her parents at the breakfast table. "I'd like to see which students will be attending the new school you're building. I know we're off for the summer, but it never hurts to spread the word."

"Anake mentioned she needed some butter," Mama said, spreading pineapple jam on a biscuit. "How many days will these extra workers be here?"

"About three." Jack speared another slice of ham. "They should be arriving at any time. I'd prefer it if you and Lucy stay out of sight as much as possible. They aren't always the most savory of characters."

There was something he wasn't telling them. The lines between his eyes weren't disappearing with breakfast. Lucy watched him over the rim of her coffee mug. Why would something that happened every year bring him worry?

She wanted to dig into the matter, but needed to get moving if she wanted to visit even half of the homes in the area. Jack had already offered her the use of the mare whenever she needed her. Now that her hands were healed, it was time to get back to the real reason she was on the island. To teach the children English and about how much God loves them. Jack is an extra bonus, another incentive to cause her to want to make her home there.

After collecting her reticule and making sure she looked her best, she left her mother and Anake to work their magic in the kitchen and headed to the barn to see if someone would help her saddle the mare. She really needed to learn to do such things herself. Especially since she had no plans on living anywhere else.

The stableboy glanced repeatedly at her from under the wide brimmed hat he wore as he saddled the horse. Lucy took a handkerchief from her reticule and wiped her face. Did she have a smudge? Was her hair falling loose?

The moment the horse was ready, the boy skedaddled outside as if Lucy had the plague. She shrugged and led the mare to a stool in order for her to climb into the saddle. The sun was quickly rising to the noon hour, and she not only needed to visit students, but stop by her rented apartment and spend some time trying to sell to tourists. That little money making plan had quickly been forgotten in the excitement of the fire, and rent would be due in a few days. Suddenly, the day wasn't long enough for all Lucy had to do.

She stopped in front of her shop. Within minutes, she had an easel and fresh sketchpad set up and started drawing the tourists mingling up and down the street. One little girl in particular, wearing a bright pink dress and a floppy hat, caught her attention as she leaned over and stared into the well. Lucy sketched the scene in pencil, then colored in only the child's dress and hat ribbon.

"That is beautiful." The child's mother peered over Lucy's shoulder. "How much?"

"One dollar." Lucy handed over the drawing. Having now attracted the attention of multiple tourists who wanted their children's portraits, it was late afternoon before she closed up shop. If she tarried much longer, she'd be visiting homes at the dinner hour, which was never the polite thing to do.

She climbed back into the saddle and headed away from the main section of town. The warm afternoon and lush foliage made her want to stop and enjoy the day. Still, duty called, her pockets jingled with coins, and she had Jack to head back to later that evening.

She eyed the lowering sun with trepidation. If she didn't hurry, they'd send someone looking for her, and Mama would lecture. She urged the horse into a trot as a light rain began to fall.

After the third door slammed in her face, Lucy suspected something was wrong. It wasn't that everyone was rude, exactly, but more like they were afraid to talk to her. Why? She stood in the yard of the last home for the day and glanced up and down a road that was eerily silent.

The hair on the back of her neck prickled. If there was something to be feared, wouldn't the military be scouting the area? Shouldn't she see at least one jeep rumbling past if there was something to be concerned about?

Still, she couldn't shake the feeling that something was going to change, and not for the better. She hurried to her horse. Normally, she wouldn't think twice about being out after dark in the peaceful community, but her instincts practically screamed for her to get home, and fast.

The rain had increased, the wind ripped her hat from her head. Still, she hurried to the ranch, wanting nothing more than to see the faces of her loved ones and know that everyone was all right. It wasn't a storm she feared, she wasn't sure exactly what had her nerves on edge, but she breathed a sigh of relief to see Mama waiting on the front porch.

"Lucy, you are a sight."

"I'm sorry. I've had the strangest day." Lucy handed the horse's reins to the stableboy. "Normally friendly people were very unresponsive today. I did manage to sell a few portraits, but …" she shrugged. "Something told me to hurry home."

"Mr. Garrison and his foreman have been in the bunkhouse with the new hired hands for hours now. They've both missed the dinner bell, and Anake is as skittish as a colt. It was good for you to hurry." Mama glanced toward the sea. "I thought maybe a storm—"

"I did, too, at first. But the clouds are staying put. Where is Papa?"

"He isn't home yet. You go ahead and get your dinner. I'm going to sit out here a while."

"I'll bring you a plate, and we'll wait together."

~

Jack stared at the room of sullen workers. They'd arrived almost a day late and done nothing but argue and make demands. Not in the almost ten years since running the ranch without his father, had he run across such a group of men unwilling to do any work for a high rate of pay. "I'm paying you more than a standard wage for three full days of your hard work. I don't see how that is any reason to complain. I've used this group every year and had no complaints before."

Juan, the head of the group, stepped forward. "That's before rich people took over the island. Not only that, but missionaries come and tell us our way of worship is wrong. We won't have it!"

What did that have to do with the circumstances at hand? "I'm sorry you feel that way, but I am not one of the people trying to enslave you. I've built this ranch, after the death of my family, by the sweat of my brow. I'm no different than you."

"Ha! That hat you wear would feed my family for a week."

Jack ripped the hat off his head and threw it at the man's feet. "Then sell it and feed your family. Either you get to work or you don't get paid. I've twenty head of cattle that need rounding up and branded. Breakfast is at six." He stormed from the bunkhouse, stopping when he spotted Lucy and Mrs. Dillow on the lanai. Their serious expressions told him they were worried about something.

"Is everything all right?" He propped one booted foot on the step.

"Papa hasn't come home yet." Lucy's eyes shimmered in the moonlight.

"He's hours past due." Mrs. Dillow stared over Jack's shoulder at the darkness.

Jack's heart rate accelerated. With the upheaval

concerning the workers, could Mr. Dillow have met with trouble? "Where did he go?"

"To minister to a man whose wife died in the night." Mrs. Dillow twisted her skirt in her hands. "Oh, Mr. Garrison, that was this morning."

"I'll find him." He marched into the house and to the cabinet where he kept his pistol. With little reason to carry a gun on the island, he kept the revolver put away most of the time. His gut told him this was not one of those times.

After explaining the situation to Anake, he headed back to the porch. "You two get inside, please. Don't come out for anyone but me or Mr. Dillow."

"What's happening?" Lucy bolted to her feet.

"Just do as I ask." Jack planted a kiss on her cheek, gave a nod to Mrs. Dillow, and went to retrieve his horse from the barn.

It wouldn't be hard to find out who had died last night. He would begin his search for Mr. Dillow there. In the saddle, he urged the horse into the fastest pace that was safe in the dark.

His first stop was the dry goods store owner. "Why, sure," she said. "I know it was Bertie Hayes that died last night. She's that sweet woman who moved from the mainland last year. Do you know her? She's been sick for quiet a while, you know."

"Thank you." He did know where the Hayes lived, and turned in the direction of the Volcano House. After visiting the island and staying in the lush surroundings of the island's most popular hotel, the Hayes had purchased a small cottage down the road.

He stopped in front of the cottage and climbed from the saddle, leaving the horse to graze on a patch of thick grass. A single candle burned in the front window. It didn't look as if Mr. Dillow was there, but Jack couldn't leave without exhausting all avenues.

He rapped on the door and stood back while a grieving Mr. Hayes, a man well into his sixties, opened the door. "Mr. Garrison?"

"I'm sorry for your loss, Mr. Hayes. Please let me know if there is anything I can do." Jack shifted from one foot to the other. Since the death of his family, consequences such as this one left him uncomfortable.

"I'm heading back to the mainland in a couple of days, but thank you."

"I heard that Mr. Dillow was here?"

"Yes. He's a very kind man. Stayed for several hours and booked passage on a ship for me. He left before dinner."

Several hours again? Jack again expressed his condolences then turned to scan up and down the road. Where had Lucy's father gone after leaving here? He got back on his horse and rode slowly in the direction of the ranch, watching the thick foliage on each side of the road for any sign of the man. He couldn't bear to face Lucy if he returned without her father.

He'd ridden approximately a mile before spotting something white behind a thick bush. He slid from the saddle and slid down the embankment to find Mr. Dillow bleeding from a head wound and holding his side.

"Thank God you found me," he said. "I don't think I can make it home on my own."

"What happened?" Jack helped him to his feet, and keeping one arm around his waist, helped him to the horse. The head wound continued to bleed, staining Mr. Dillow's white shirt dark.

"I was on my way home from seeing a friend and was waylaid. The cowards jumped me from behind and robbed me of my last two dollars." He gripped the saddle horn.

Jack helped heft him into the saddle and swung up behind him. "That type of thing doesn't usually happen here."

"There's a lot of talk in the village about some discontented hired hands at your ranch. They seem bent on stirring up trouble. Now, I'm not saying they're the ones who mugged me, but it's a good guess. A missionary is a very unpopular person right now."

"Let's get you home and safe. I don't want any of you leaving the house for the next three days. They'll be gone by then. If I could get the work done without them, I'd send them packing."

"No worries, son. I'm fine and will heed your advice." While he tried to remain upright, Mr. Dillow groaned and slumped against Jack's chest. "My apologies, but I can't seem to hold my head up."

"Lean against me. I can hold you." Jack kicked the horse into a faster gait, hoping he wasn't costing the man more pain. But, the head wound bothered him. It needed bandaging, and fast, not to mention he might have a cracked rib or two.

The moment they stopped in front of the house, Lucy and her mother dashed outside. "What happened?" Mrs. Dillow reached for her husband.

"Robbery." Jack helped Mr. Dillow to the ground and supported his weight as the women followed them into the house. "Anake! Bandages for a head wound and possible busted ribs."

She nodded around the corner of the kitchen and bustled away.

"Don't worry, Mrs. Dillow. He's in good hands. Anake is a marvelous nurse."

"I'm beginning to think there isn't anything that woman can't do."

"I haven't found anything." Jack forced a smile in an attempt to ease the creases in her forehead.

"Don't worry the women about the workers," Mr. Dillow whispered as Jack helped him to bed. "It won't accomplish anything."

"If you wish." If they stayed inside as Jack ordered, there would be no reason to tell them. Although, knowing Lucy as he did, he didn't think she would stay inside without an explanation. The Dillow women were stronger than Mr. Dillow gave them credit for. "But, we will have to tell them something."

"Tell them there are dangerous men afoot, but not that those men are possibly living here. My wife will have a nervous breakdown." He hissed as Jack helped him lie flat.

"I'll help him now." Mrs. Dillow rushed into the room with a bowl of water and a rag. "Oh, dear. That cut will require stitches."

"I'll go for the doctor." Jack spun and rushed

past Lucy.

She grabbed his arm to stop him. "What is going on?" Her eyes flashed. "You can't tell us to stay inside, bring my father home in this condition, and not expect me to ask questions."

"You're right." He pulled her into the privacy of the dining room. "Your father asked that I not say anything, but you deserve to know." He put his hands on her shoulders and stared into her eyes. "The new men I've hired resent the appearance of missionaries on the island."

14

When Lucy walked into the living room, Papa jerked, almost knocking the book on his lap onto the floor.

Lucy steadied it. "Jack told me about the unhappy workers. I won't take any unnecessary chances. How are you feeling today?" Lucy set a breakfast tray on his lap and bent to peer closer at his head wound. "Anake was a marvel stitching you up."

"That she was." He leaned forward so Lucy could put another pillow behind him. "But, she wrapped my ribs so tight I can hardly breathe, or move."

"Don't be so grumpy. You'll most likely heal faster because of her ministrations. Would you like me to go to the base and fetch the army medic?"

"No!" He paled.

"I asked Mr. Garrison not to do that." Papa shook his head. "I'm fine as I am."

"It seems Jack thinks me more capable of handling news than you do." Lucy sat in the chair next to the sofa and motioned for him to eat. "When will you realize that I am no longer a child?"

"I realized that the moment Mr. Garrison came to me stating his intentions toward you."

Her throat clogged. "And still you withheld your blessing."

"Your mother and I only desire that you understand what you would be getting yourself into."

"I understand quite well." She crossed her arms and leaned back. "Mama also told me of what the two of you went through before you married. Why is this so different? If you say it is because of Jack's native blood, I march from this room immediately."

"No, I won't—" He stopped as Jack entered the room.

"I'm heading to the summer pasture and taking the men with me." His dark gaze landed on Lucy, his look warm enough to heat her blood. "I'd like to request that you stay close to the house as you go about your errands."

Lucy nodded. "I'll go no further than I need to in order to collect the eggs."

"Thank you." He turned to Papa and gave a nod. "It's good to see you up and eating, sir. I leave the ladies in your capable hands." With a tender smile at Lucy, he turned and hurried from the room.

Papa sighed. "I've lost, haven't I?"

She laughed and planted a kiss on his cheek. "You had no chance of winning, you dear old man."

"I suppose." He took her hand. "Pray, that's all I ask."

"I haven't stopped." She gave his hand a squeeze and pulled away. "I've work to do. I'll come check on you in a bit."

"I can handle your father." Mama breezed into the room and frowned at the almost full plate of pancakes. "Eat."

"Yes, dear."

Lucy grinned and removed the egg basket from its hook by the door. Papa was in good, if not bossy, hands with Mama and Anake.

The bright morning sun greeted her as soon as she stepped off the lanai. On the horizon, indigo clouds formed, promising rain later in the day. She closed her eyes and took a deep breath of air laden with the aroma of the ocean. She could never tire of such a place. Not even Jack's warning could cast a pall over such a glorious day.

The basket swinging from her fingers, she headed to the thick beach grass and began her search for tomorrow's breakfast. Somewhere, a dog barked, followed by the shriek of laughter from a child. Lucy's smile grew along with the amount of eggs she collected. Someday, it would be her child playing on the beach while she joined in, running hand-in-hand along the water's edge. Jack was part of the happy picture, the dark haired child between them.

She glanced at Kilauea. Who would have guessed such a temperamental mountain would bring Lucy the man she loved?

She set the basket on the sand and sat down to remove her shoes. A little time spent in the surf wouldn't delay morning chores for too long. She left her shoes and stockings beside the basket and ran with abandon to the water, soaking the hem of her pale blue skirt. Mama would lecture, but Lucy was beginning to think that perhaps Mama was a tiny bit jealous of Lucy's ability to seize fun where she could. She'd bring her with her later and insist she splash around for a few minutes.

A not so gentle bump to her backside sent her stumbling forward. Her arms windmilled. She went down with a splash, swallowing sea water. She struggled to her feet to find out the culprit was a young calf.

"Where is your mother, you naughty thing." She reached a hand toward the animal's nose, only to have the calf take a step back.

"Aloha." A man she didn't recognize grinned from the beach. "It's a nice day for a swim."

Lucy scanned the area, looking for Jack. Was this one of his workers? The calf had to be one of Jack's. How many ranchers resided on the main island?

"Aloha." She splashed a few feet away and emerged from the sea.

"You are like a mermaid, coming to entice me to a watery grave."

"Very poetic, but I must return home." She glanced around for her basket.

It swung from the man's hands. Her mouth dried like the beach grass. She was a fool for coming out alone.

"Are you looking for this?" He grinned, revealing a missing front tooth.

The breeze shifted, carrying the stench of whiskey with it. Barely noon, and the man was obviously drunk.

"Those are my eggs. May I have them,

please?"

"Come and get them, my little mermaid."

Her heart pounded so hard, she feared he would see her fear. She lifted her chin, determined to remain brave. "I am not your anything." She held out her hand. " The eggs, please. Where is Mr. Garrison?"

He shrugged. "Working, like the other mindless minions that follow him." He spit and tossed the eggs to the ground. His eyes narrowed.

For several long seconds, their gazes clashed, then the man lunged, grabbing Lucy's arm. She squealed and tried to twist free as he pulled her closer.

"I guess you think you're too good for the likes of me." His breath washed over her.

She averted her face and tried not to gag. Glancing up the embankment, she prayed for a sight of her mother or Anake. Surely, one of them wondered where she was.

"Shouldn't you return the calf?" A different tactic other than fighting might work. If the man thought she wasn't completely repulsed by him, he might loosen his grip. "Did Mr. Garrison send you looking for it?"

His face darkened. "I'm not at his beck and call." He tried snaking his arm around her. "A girl as pretty as you must be different from the other mainlanders. You don't dress like one of the rich. I've heard stories of how you help the children, trying to teach them English. Isn't their native tongue good enough for you?"

"Of course it is." She yanked harder. "But it's

beneficial to everyone to be bilingual. Why, I bet a man as smart as you knows more than one language."

"I know three." His chest puffed. "I aim to be an important man someday. The name of Juan will be one of respect."

Lucy took advantage of his boasting, brought her elbow up to his nose with a satisfying crunch. He howled and released her. Hitching her skirt above her knees, she dashed down the beach.

Pounding footsteps alerted her to her pursuer. She veered for a cliff surrounded by craggy rocks. If she could find a place to hide, the man would forget about her and go back to the calf. She hoped. At the very least, he might stumble in his inebriated state and give her time to get away.

Unmindful of the coral biting into her hands and feet, she scrambled over the rocks. There! A crack in the wall. A glance over her shoulder showed he still pursued her, although unsteadily. She increased her pace, squeezing between a gap in the cliff wall.

Her breath came in gasps. The sandy floor, covered in salt spray, stung the cuts on her feet. The man called for her, still using the term of her being his mermaid.

"Have you gone to sea, Mermaid?" He yelped, then cursed. "I will find you. Tomorrow. I'll find you tomorrow."

Lucy closed her eyes and leaned her head against the rock wall.

"Or today. I will sit here and rest until you come out."

She clapped a hand over her mouth to stifle a cry. How long will he wait? Oh, Mama and Papa would be so worried. Even at that moment, they probably looked for her. The knowledge gave her hope. All she had to do was bide her time until the man left, or she was found.

She slid to the ground, her wet skirt tangling around her legs. Wrapping her arms around her knees, she prepared to wait. A cool wind blew, chilling her. The storm. How could she have forgotten?

The walls around her showed signs of water. What if she were stuck inside the cave during high tide? There. A small ledge would keep her safe.

She pushed to her feet and peered outside. Juan snored, propped against a boulder like a piece of driftwood. If she were quiet, she could sneak past him, and … Her foot dislodged a pebble, sending it clattering across the coral.

"Mermaid?"

Lucy gasped and clamored onto the ledge. It looked as if she would be stuck for a while. Tears spilled down her cheeks as she wrapped her scraped hands in the folds of her skirt. She closed her eyes and prayed for rescue. *Oh, Jack, come find me.*

~

Irresponsible Juan! Jack hung his horse's saddle over the pony wall in the barn. He'd sent the man after a wayward calf hours ago. He hadn't missed the stench of whiskey on his breath, but thought he could handle a simple task.

He stepped from the barn to see Anake and Mrs. Dillow trudging across the lawn despite the heavy downpour and heavy winds of the storm. Spotting him, they both broke into a run.

"Jack." Anake thrust an empty basket at him. "Lucy is missing. We've looked everywhere. All we found was the egg basket and shattered eggs."

Mrs. Dillow raised red-rimmed eyes. "You must find her."

His heart dropped to his boots. Missing? "How long has she been gone?"

"Since this morning." Anake hung her head. "We didn't search for a couple of hours, not thinking anything was amiss. She had a long list of chores to do. We merely thought her busy."

"Bring me my slicker." Jack traded his favorite hat for one more waterproof. Where could the silly woman have gone? "Did anyone check her room in town? Perhaps she went to sell some more drawings and decided to stay when the storm blew in."

"No, we didn't." Mrs. Dillow's face brightened. "I'm sure that's what happened."

It was possible, despite Jack's orders to remain at the ranch. She could have thought herself safe enough surrounded by tourists. "I'll check there first. Have hot coffee ready when we return. We'll be wet and cold. If one of you could make sure the hired hands are fed, I'd appreciate it." He was going to wring her little neck when he found her.

"Let me get you some food to take with you." Anake raced for the house.

"Do you really think she's in town?" Mrs. Dillow clutched his arm.

"Sure." He forced a smile. Lucy could be anywhere, but he wouldn't worry her mother further. "We'll be back before you know it." He wouldn't return without her.

He turned back to saddle his horse, almost bumping into Manuel, who had entered behind him. "Juan is gone, too," he said. "One of the other men found the calf wandering the beach. Do you think he has drowned in his drunken state?"

"I can't worry about Juan right now. If someone else wants to look for him, they are free to do so." He slung the saddle onto his horse's back, feeling sorry that he had to take the animal back out into the weather. "Just don't let anyone head out alone."

"You are going alone."

Jack sighed. "Yes, I am, but the fewer exposed to this storm, the better. I know my way around the island."

"Be careful." Manuel headed through the rain to the bunkhouse as Jack led his horse outside.

Anake returned, drenched, with his slicker and a pail containing a canteen and several wrapped sandwiches. "I've wrapped the food in greased paper. Maybe they will stay dry."

"Thank you." He slipped into the slicker, buttoned it to his chin and slapped his hat on his head before swinging into the saddle. "Sorry, old boy, but there's a lady that needs to be found." He trotted toward the village, hoping, praying, that Lucy had done what he told her mother was likely.

Rain dripped off the brim of his hat and ran in rivulets down the back of his raincoat. No one traveled the road, not on a day as wet as this one. Heavy clouds covered the sun. Only the growling of his stomach told Jack it neared suppertime.

Lucy's shop in the village was dark. One glance through the window told him she wasn't there. Where did he look now? He glanced toward their favorite beach. She wouldn't have gone that far. If she had decided to get her feet wet, she would have chosen the beach behind the ranch house. He had wasted valuable time coming to the village.

"Mr. Garrison?" Hank, the native owner of a small diner, opened his door. "What brings you out on such a day?"

"Lucy Dillow, the missionary's daughter, has been missing since morning. We're worried something bad had happened to her." Jack tilted back his hat. "Have you had any trouble in town today?"

He shook his head. "Some rumors of men wanting to start something, but that's all they are, just rumors. You keep looking, sir, and I'll see who I can round up to help. We all love that young woman. The world needs more just like her."

"Thank you." His neighbors really were the best people.

The more he rode, the more dread filled him. If she had met with an accident and fallen into the ocean ... No, he wouldn't think that way. Lucy was safe from the storm unless evidence proved otherwise. He had to believe that.

He glanced heavenward. *God, can you hear me? I know we haven't been regular correspondents, but I need your help here. Please, let me find Lucy, alive and well.* He tugged his collar higher around his ears and headed back in the direction of the ranch.

Instead of entering the yard, he steered the horse into a patch of jungle, sheltering it in the trees before heading in the direction of the beach. His mind replayed the information he had.

Lucy had gone for eggs. The empty basket and crushed eggs were found on the beach, thus Lucy had been on the beach at some point. Any footprints would have long been washed away. His spirits sank. Finding her in a short amount of time didn't look promising.

Waves crashed against the small amount of beach left after high tide. To Jack's right, villagers swarmed the small hill, calling Lucy's name. Their efforts warmed him, despite the rain running down his collar. If she was here, they would find her.

"Lucy!" The wind ripped her name from his lips and carried it over the island.

"Over here!" Someone shouted.

Jack ran to where they pointed. Lying among the rocks was a very wet and unconscious Juan. Jack grabbed him by the shirt and dragged him a safer distance from the water. He slapped his frigid cheeks. "Wake up, man."

"Mermaid?"

"He's delusional," a man said over Jack's shoulder.

Juan shook his head. "I saw her come from the sea, all dark hair and silky like a seal."

Was he talking about Lucy? "Where?"

"She's gone. Disappeared with the waves." His eyes fluttered. "I chased her, but she eluded me, my mermaid."

Jack shook him. "Open your eyes and tell me where Lucy Dillow is." Jack released him, letting him fall to the grass.

He cupped his hands around his mouth and called her name. If Juan had harmed her, Jack would throttle him with his bare hands. He turned back to the man. "Where is she!?"

"The rocks. She disappeared in the rocks." Juan rolled over, curling into himself. "It's cold, man, have pity."

Jack restrained himself from kicking him and glanced to where Juan said Lucy had gone. Waves slapped at the cliffs, covering the reef that was normally exposed. If she'd gone that way, she had little chance of survival.

"Where's my daughter?" Mr. Dillow, his arms wrapped around his middle, stood by Jack's side.

"You shouldn't be out here in your condition." Jack continued staring at the cliffs.

"I have as much right as you do."

"Please." He cut him a sideways glance. "I can't watch you and look for Lucy."

"I'll take care of myself." He swayed.

Jack huffed and helped him sit on a patch of grass. "If you further injure yourself, you're taking full responsibility."

"We're here, boss." Manuel, followed by several regular ranch hands, hurried across the small strip of beach not pounded by the waves.

"Thank you." Jack clasped his hands. "I'm heading for those rocks."

"That's suicide."

"Juan mentioned a mermaid. I can only assume

he meant Lucy." He dropped his slicker and tugged off his boots. "Maybe she found a place to hide out of the weather."

"There is no such place." Manuel stepped in front of him. "You grew up here. You know there is nothing there."

Jack stripped down to only his pants. "I'm going to look."

He met Mr. Dillow's wide-eyed gaze. Neither of them said anything, but knowing the futility of his search. "Pray, Mr. Dillow."

He nodded, clasping his hands in his lap. Jack turned and sprinted for the rocks. He had to find her. She was resourceful. If there was anywhere to go, she would find it. He had to keep a tight hold on believing that.

A wave slammed into him, knocking him off his feet. He took a deep breath as he went over, losing his air when he crashed into the reef. He fought his way to the surface, ignoring the pain in his side and wrapped his arms around the thick root of a bush struggling to survive on the cliff face.

No one could survive out here, much less a woman encumbered by her skirts. The force of the waves was almost too much for Jack. His arms felt as if they were being torn from their sockets. Salt water blinded him. Rough rocks scraped his skin. What had Lucy endured to escape Juan, if she had indeed come this way?

He took another deep breath as a wave broke over his head. When he came up, he spotted it. A thin crevice in the cave wall. "Lucy!"

15

Lucy lifted her head off her knees and opened her eyes. Sleep tugged at her like the waves against the shore. She'd heard something over the crash of water surging into the cave. There it was again. "Jack!" She eyed the water below the ledge she had taken refuge on. Already freezing, she was afraid if she were to slip into the water, her legs would no longer hold her up.

"I'm in here." Praying he could hear her, she struggled to stand, her feet stinging from cuts and cold. She knew he'd come for her.

His arm waved through the crack she'd slipped through, followed by one side of his face. "My shoulders won't fit. You'll have to come to me." He grunted and disappeared.

He was being battered to death, and she could only stare at the water she knew was over her head. "Are you there?"

"I'm here, but you've got to hurry, sweetheart. It's getting worse out here. I don't know how much longer I can hold on."

Lucy took a deep breath and jumped. Her nose filled with salt water as the cold took her breath away. She fought against her skirt dragging her down until her head cleared the surface. She gasped. "I'm coming."

"No," he yelled from outside. "Stay there. I can't hold on."

Please, hold on. She stretched out her hand, missing as Jack disappeared again and the tide carried her away from the opening. Again, she fought the tide, until her fingers grasped the rough surface of the cave entrance. She kicked harder, sliding through and out into the worst storm she had encountered since arriving on the island.

Where was Jack? She plastered herself against the cliff and squinted against the driving rain. His head broke the surface on the other side of the rocks. She screamed his name so he could find her.

He glanced her way, then, with long strokes, made his way toward her. With every stroke he made her way, he was pushed back two. Lucy pushed away from the cliff and let the water carry her to him.

"What are you doing?" He wrapped his arms around her, his lips against her ear. "You were safer where you were. I was a fool to ask you to come to me."

"I won't let you go. We'll do this together." Even if that meant dying. She wasn't going to let him be pushed out to sea because she had decided to take a walk on the beach that afternoon. A decision that had gone against his advice and gotten her into a lot of trouble.

They bobbed like pieces of driftwood. Lucy's skirt tangled around their legs like seaweed. Together, they managed to make their way to a place in the reef that formed a half-moon. It kept them from being swept out to sea, but did nothing to protect them from the wind and surf. Each wave slammed them into the rocks until Lucy feared no part of her body was going to be left uncut and unbruised.

"Here." Manuel tossed them a rope, stepping onto the reef and putting himself in danger. "We'll pull you in." Several other workers from the ranch joined him.

"Hold tight," Jack said, grabbing the rope. "The rocks won't feel good." He wrapped the rope around their waists, lashing her tightly to him before giving his foreman the signal for the men to start tugging them to shore.

Lucy grit her teeth against the further pain of banging against the rocks, finally releasing a shuddering breath when she felt firm ground under her. She lay against Jack as they were untied.

"You saved me." Tears mingled with the sea water and raindrops on her face. "Oh, Jack, look at you."

There was not an inch of his back and arms that weren't scraped raw from the rocks. Because of her, he lay injured and in pain, again. She forgot about her own scrapes as she caressed his face.

"Come, daughter. Let his men tend to him." Papa helped her to her feet. "We need to get the both of you home." He helped her to a wagon someone had brought. In the back, snored Juan.

"I will not ride with that man." She glared. "I'd rather walk on my bleeding feet, than share a wagon with him.

"Get out." Jack stood next to her and slapped Juan's booted foot. "Now."

The man's eyes popped open. He took one look at Jack and Lucy and scampered from the wagon. Manuel and the others immediately surrounded him.

Jack held out his hand to help Lucy into the wagon bed. With the help of Papa, he climbed in beside her. He took a long glance at Lucy, shook his head, and lay against the back of the wagon. "We'll talk later."

He was furious with her, and rightly so. She sighed and slouched against the wood. Would he no longer want a future with her? Not that she blamed him. What kind of woman put the man she loved in danger as Lucy had? Not to mention the worry she had caused her parents. All because she desired a stroll along the beach and couldn't wait another couple of days for the hired hands to leave the island.

Mama was right. Lucy didn't belong here. Only a place such as a town in the middle of the continent would be safe enough for her. She tried pushing aside the avalanche of self-pity, but it was hard when Jack lay bleeding beside her, and her hands and feet felt as if they were on fire.

"Are you all right, daughter?" Papa climbed in beside her.

She nodded. "As well as can be expected."

He patted her shoulder. "You'll be better with dry clothes and something to eat."

"Most likely." Although, it was a lie. Knowing she'd made the decision to leave the island with her parents in a few months, cast a shadow over the days ahead. Somehow, she needed to find a way to convince Jack that her decision was sound.

Mama and Anake waited on the lanai when they stopped in front of the house. Manuel and the others ushered Juan to the barn while Lucy and Jack handed themselves over to the ministrations of the women.

Within half an hour, once again dressed in one of Anake's voluminous muumuus, Lucy sat at the kitchen table, a cup of hot coffee warming her hands. Jack, wearing a clean white shirt, sat across from her.

"Thank you," Lucy said, staring into her cup. "For saving my life, again."

"Why didn't you listen to me? I told you to stay close." He put a hand over hers. "I said that to keep you safe."

She nodded. "I know. The water was so inviting, and I thought all the workers had gone with you. It didn't occur to me that one would return for some reason." She raised her eyes, looking at him through a shimmer of tears. "I didn't mean to almost get you killed."

"Not just me, Lucy, but yourself. Getting caught in a hidden cave at high tide," his throat moved as he swallowed. "I might never have found you. You could have died and been there forever."

"I'm sorry."

"Enough of that." Mama set a plate of scrambled eggs in front of each of them. "Eat and go to bed. This conversation can take place tomorrow."

Lucy agreed. Exhaustion coated her like the

ash of the volcano had filled the air, choking her, weighing her down. After a long sleep, she would be in better condition to break the news of her leaving to Jack. They could have no future together without trust, and how could he trust her now?

"Thank you again." She stood, made a move to touch him, then pulled back. "Goodnight."

He grabbed her hand. "What are you not telling me? Did something happen out there with … Juan?"

"No. I got away in time." She caressed his face with her eyes. "We'll talk in the morning. Please? I'm so very tired."

A shadow crossed his face. His look turned sad, breaking her heart. "Tomorrow, then. When I return from working with the cattle."

"You're in no shape to work."

He shoved back his chair. "I have a feeling that after our conversation tomorrow, your opinion as to what I can and cannot do, will no longer be welcome." He set his lips firmly and marched from the room, leaving her heart in shattered pieces on the floor.

~

What had happened to cause Lucy to change toward him. Yesterday, she'd been loving and warm. Now, after he'd rescued her from the ocean, she had turned as cold as a fish. Instead of heading for his room, he sat out on the lanai.

His heart told him she was going to leave the island, and that's what she wanted to talk to him about. He wouldn't let her. He'd profess his love and make her stay. Once she heard how much he loves her, she won't be able to go.

Loud voices from the direction of the barn interrupted his thoughts. He reached through the open front door of the house and grabbed his gun someone had thought to bring along with the clothes he had discarded on the beach. With a groan, he set off to the barn, his body protesting each step of the way.

He stopped at the big double doors. The Filipino hands, minus Juan, who was tied up in the corner and sporting a bloody lip, faced off with Jack's regular hands. From the body language on both sides, a fight was in the making.

"What's going on?" Keeping his weapon in plain sight, he moved to Manuel's side.

"We were teaching this piece of sea garbage a lesson, when his friends decided to intervene." Manuel clenched his fists. "Said a missionary girl wasn't worth the time it was going to take to get Juan to the authorities."

"That's no excuse for what's happening here. We have one more day of working together. I'll send someone to take Juan." He glanced around the group. "I've had a long day. My body hurts. I want nothing more than to go to bed, but I can't do that if I have to worry about you imbeciles wrecking my ranch or beating each other up to where you can't work. Are we going to settle down, or do I need to sleep out here in the hay?"

"We're good, boss." Manuel nodded and glared at the other workers. Slowly, they all nodded in return.

"Good. No one else lays a hand on Juan." He whirled and marched from the barn. Not that he didn't want to choke the living daylights out of the man. His drunken escapade on the beach could have resulted in Lucy's death. Jack wasn't sure he would have been able to rein in his temper had that happened.

So much for a peaceful half hour on the lanai. He headed to the back of the house and his bed.

As soft as his sheets were, they still rubbed against his scrapes, keeping him awake. Add his physical discomfort to his heartache, and sleep wasn't going to come soon, if ever.

The creak of a door down the hall alerted him to the fact someone else couldn't sleep. Most likely, it was Lucy or her father. Jack had cracked his ribs once and found lying flat to be uncomfortable. Add in how worried her father had been that day, and most likely there were several minds that, while grateful, spun with ideas of what could have happened.

Giving up any pretense of sleep, Jack tossed aside his sheet and made his way to the kitchen, not surprised to see Mr. Dillow pouring himself the last of the coffee.

"I can make some more if you want some," he said.

Jack shook his head. "Couldn't sleep either, huh?"

"No." He pulled a chair away from the table and sat. "It was a brave thing you did today, jumping into the ocean with no idea of where Lucy was. You both could have drowned."

"We almost did." He shuddered, thinking of the fierceness of the storm.

"You're a brave man, and I am in your debt for the rest of my life." Mr. Dillow stared into his cup.

"I couldn't do anything other than look for her, Mr. Dillow."

"I suppose you couldn't." He glanced up, his gaze meeting Jack's. "I can't think of a better man to marry my daughter to."

Emotions flooded through him, and he blinked back tears. "I fear Lucy has changed her mind about marrying me."

"Have you actually proposed to my daughter?"

"No. I wanted your blessing first. It was more like an unspoken agreement." Could it be that simple? Jack thought she knew of his feelings for her, but maybe he was mistaken. Did women want to hear declarations of love rather than move ahead on feelings? What an idiot he was. "I was starting to think she no longer wanted to stay on the island."

"That would be unfortunate." Mr. Dillow grinned. "The wife and I have decided to stay and pastor the church you are building." He folded his hands around his mug. "Lucy has always been a dreamer and as stubborn as her mother. If you want to know what she is thinking, you have got to get her to tell you, and don't stop pressing the issue until you're satisfied. Don't take no for an answer, Mr. Garrison. My girl loves you. Of that I have no doubt."

"Please, sir, call me Jack." The last thing Jack wanted to do in the next few hours was hunt wayward cattle. Not when a serious conversation needed to be carried on between him and Lucy. "You don't think your daughter is feeling a bit of guilt for not following my orders?"

He laughed. "Oh, I know she's feeling a lot of guilt. If she's been cold toward you, that's the reason. She endangered you because of her own selfish desires. That will haunt her for days."

The clock on the mantel struck midnight. Mr. Dillow stood and set his cup in the sink. "It's time for me to retire for the night." He smiled. "Don't fret about Lucy. She'll be here when work is finished tomorrow. I doubt she'll set foot off your property for days to come. If she does want to go to the village, I'll be sure to accompany her."

"Thank you." Jack waited until the man went to his room before heading back to the lanai. The storm had passed, leaving the air cool and heavy with moisture.

At least Mr. Dillow no longer had any reservations about Lucy marrying an islander. That alone was worth the jump into the sea.

He sat in one of the rockers and propped his feet on the railing. He should purchase a hammock for nights like this where sleeping outside was preferable to inside. He leaned his head back and closed his eyes, willing his body to relax and ignore the throbbing of bruises.

Not only had Jack saved Lucy, but she had saved him the moment he first set eyes on her. If not for her and her stubborn need to study the volcano, he would have been content to remain a bachelor, lonely and unloved except for Anake. God had given him a gift in Lucy, one he hadn't known he needed.

After the death of his family, Jack never

wanted to risk his heart again. Still, he'd given it into the hands of a mainlander, and almost lost it in the sea. He grinned in the dark. He'd do it again if only to prove to Lucy's parents how much she meant to him.

A cow mooed, reminding Jack of another long day of work in a few hours. Despite Juan's laziness, they'd managed to bring in most of the cattle, leaving one more day of work instead of two. Jack would pay the hands for three days, as agreed, and look elsewhere next year for help. Either a man wanted an honest day's wage or they weren't worth the headache.

"Papa?" Lucy's voice drifted through the open window.

Did she seek his advice as Jack had? Would Mr. Dillow tell her of their conversation? Jack hoped not. He didn't want anything to sway Lucy's decision, other than the words he spoke to her.Her father murmured something back to her, followed by whispers from her mother. Lucy said something else before Jack heard the shutting of a door. He closed his eyes, prepared to get a few hours of sleep before Anake woke him for breakfast. The day promised to be a full one.

16

Papa smiled at Lucy across the kitchen table the next morning. When she caught him, he transferred his attention to the coffee in front of him, his smile not dimming.

Something was definitely not right. Mama and Anake were whispering behind closed doors and Papa resembled the porpoise she'd once seen off the coast of California. Jack had left earlier for the last of the cattle roundup, so he couldn't be a source of their entertainment. Lucy must have done something the rest thought quite comical.

"I'm taking my coffee to the lanai." She stormed outside as her father called out for her to remain close, as if she didn't learn her lesson the day before. Her body still protested with every movement. A reminder of her stubbornness and selfishness. A reminder of why she couldn't subject Jack to marriage with a woman who risked his life, not once, but twice. He deserved someone who would listen to him and realize he knew what was best, at least in regards to island life.

She sighed and sat in one of the rocking chairs. She couldn't help but envision what it would be like to sit there each evening, Jack at her side, and watch the tide roll in.

Mama, purse over her arm, stepped outside with Anake. "We're heading into the village. We should be home by lunch time."

"Wait for me. I'd love to go." Lucy stood.

"No." Mama shook her head. "You are in no condition to walk that far. Maybe tomorrow."

Lucy was taken aback. Mama had no reason to keep Lucy from going. Yes, she was asked to stay close to the house, but that was to prevent her from going anywhere alone. "I need to set up shop and sell more of my drawings."

"That reminds me." Mama pulled an envelope from her purse. "This came in yesterday's mail." She glanced at Anake, grinned, and they strolled down the walk, giggling like a couple of school girls.

Lucy ripped the envelope open. A check for fifty dollars fell into her lap along with a letter from Mr. Woodward, which stated that her drawings of the volcano explosion had been used in newspapers across the country, and he hoped the check sufficient compensation for her work.

She clasped the letter to her chest. After three months, she hadn't expected any recognition. She hadn't expected to be paid, but the money was welcomed, even at such a far away date. Especially, since she planned on moving back to the village within a few days.

"What's that?" Papa joined her, sitting in the chair next to her.

"Funds from my drawings of the explosion." She tucked the check and letter back into the envelope. "It validates what I'd done."

"You're quite talented." He patted her arm. "I recognized that when I flipped through that sketchbook of yours. Nice likeness of Mr. Garrison."

"Yes, about that—"

He held up his hand to stop her. "No need to explain. I understand perfectly."

She frowned. What was the twinkle in his eye? "If you understand something, I'd be pleased if you would explain it to me."

He chuckled. "All will be clear in time, dear."

"What is going on around here? Mama is more giddy than I've ever seen her, and you look like a cat with a secret."

"Just happy to be alive." His grin spread and he glanced over the land at the sea. "Your mother and I have decided to stay and pastor the church that Mr. Garrison will build. That should make you happy."

It would have made her ecstatic before yesterday. Now, it filled her with a deep sadness. How could she stay and see Jack every day? Avoiding him would be nearly impossible on an island. Still, she could teach at the school. Then, she'd be the spinster school teacher she was always afraid of becoming.

"That's wonderful, Papa," she forced the words from her lips. "You'll be very happy."

"I believe you will, too. All your dreams are coming true. We aren't heading to the mainland, you'll have employment here if you desire, and can spend the rest of your days in the place you love most." He set his rocker into motion. "Yes, it is a fine day indeed."

Not all of her dreams were coming true. The most important one, the one where she married a tall, handsome rancher, had crashed into shards at her feet. Papa seemed so happy with his decision, she did her best to portray the same emotion, and felt she failed miserably.

"I'm going to do some sketching with color today." She stood. "I promise to go no further than that small rise overlooking the beach."

"Make sure I can see you from the house," he replied, making her feel like a small child.

No help for it. Yesterday's fiasco and dangerous rescue had sealed her fate for weeks to come. "I will."

She fetched her sketchbook from her room and strolled for the spot she had pointed out. Finding a place to sit on a patch of grass, she placed her pad across her lap and stared at the waves, kissed with sunlight. The fin of a porpoise broke the water's surface, eliciting a smile from her. The day held beauty even with her heart heavy. While she yearned for Jack to return home, she also dreaded it. Once he did, she would have to tell him of her decision to walk away.

Without being conscious of doing so, she found she had drawn him staring at the sea, his strong form outlined by the sun. She had to stop dwelling on him. She was tempted to rip the sheet away and toss it. Instead, she finished the drawing, adding details. It was one of her best works. Tourists wouldn't hesitate to purchase it.

She set the pad aside and leaned back, bracing herself on her hands. Why hadn't Papa brought up the fact that so many of her drawings contained an image of Jack? Once so adamant against her marrying him, her father seemed to almost be pushing her into matrimony. Had Jack's bravery yesterday removed the last brick from the wall around Papa's blessing?

Laughter reached her ears and she turned to see Mama and Anake, their arms loaded with paper-wrapped parcels, approaching the house. So lost in her drawing and thoughts, Lucy hadn't noticed the passage of time. She grabbed her pad and hurried to help with lunch.

She burst into the kitchen, her gaze landing on the piles of packages. "What did you buy?"

"Supplies," Anake said.

"I'll help put them away." Lucy reached for one of the strings holding the package closed.

"No!" Her mother and Anake shouted in unison.

Lucy jerked back. "What in the world has gotten into you two? You almost scared me to death."

"We don't want you to overdo it, dear," Mama said, giving her a hug. "Go rest with your papa."

Lucy narrowed her eyes. "I'm not tired." These two were up to something and she intended to find out what. "Several of these packages look like they could contain fabric."

"Oh." Mama met Anake's wide-eyed gaze. "We, uh, are making new dresses. Yes, I've been meaning to for weeks now."

"Uh-uh." Lucy crossed her arms. "What's the occasion?"

"No reason." Mama scooped them into her arms and marched in the direction of her room.

"You shouldn't be so nosey." Anake shook a spoon at her.

"You shouldn't be so secretive." Lucy plopped into a chair. "Everyone is acting very strange today."

"It's always like this after a storm."

"Really?"

"No." Anake grinned. "I am trying to distract you."

Lucy laughed. "It isn't working."

"Ah, but you did laugh. You have been very sad." She cupped Lucy's face. "It will all be okay. Trust me."

She wasn't sure what she was supposed to trust her for, but Lucy nodded. She'd go with the flow for now. Sooner or later, someone would let the secret slip.

~

It had been a long day, but all the cattle were accounted for and branded. Jack paid the temporary workers, and rushed them off the ranch, along with Juan. Since he hadn't actually assaulted anyone, the authorities had no reason to arrest him. Jack informed the men that he would look elsewhere next year for help if their attitudes remained the same, and in no way should Juan ever set foot on his property again. There were plenty of men looking for an honest wage.

Prolonging the conversation he knew Lucy was waiting to have, he decided to curry his horse himself. He'd like to think that she would forget, but not Lucy Dillow. The woman could latch onto something like a barracuda and not let go until the issue was resolved. He smiled. Much like her father told him he needed to be with her. So be it. Jack would get down on bended knee and not take no for an answer.

Once his horse was taken care of, he hurried into the house and took his place at the dinner table. Lucy avoided his gaze upon his greeting. Instead of taking offense, Jack grinned. He'd always loved a challenge.

Conversation around the table centered on the roundup and plans for the church and school. Mrs. Dillow and Anake told of the happenings in town, raving about the way the people had come together to help rebuild. And, with the volcano still smoking, tourism was high. Everyone was in good spirits, except for Lucy.

Her beautiful face remained turned to her plate, her hazel eyes lacking their spark. Jack hoped to relight the flame once it was proper to leave the table.

After what seemed like the longest dinner in history, chairs scraped the floor as they were pushed back. Jack took Lucy's hand before she could occupy herself in the kitchen. "Walk with me, please."

She tried to tug her hand free. "I've work to do."

"No, your mother and Anake have it covered."

"You go ahead, dear," Mrs. Dillow said. "It's a beautiful evening."

Lucy sighed and narrowed her eyes. "It's as if

the lot of you are in cahoots."

"Perhaps." He led her outside and to the beach. "Let's wade."

"Oh, Jack." Her eyes shimmered with tears. "Let's not do this."

"Yes, I insist." He plopped onto the sand to remove his boots. "We can talk as we walk."

She sighed, sounding as if she were being led to do something unpleasant, but sat beside him and removed her shoes and stockings. "Everyone has lost their minds. Mama hates it when I go wading, yet she practically encouraged you to drag me out here."

"I think your mother is relaxing toward the enjoyment of this place." He held out his hand.

She grasped it, allowing him to pull her to her feet. She raised her face to his. "Jack, I—"

"Not yet." He linked her arm with his and led her to the water's edge. "You promised me a walk first." If he could help it, he wouldn't let her tell him how she no longer loved him. He refused to believe it, but if the words were spoken out loud, they could never be taken back. He needed to tell her of his love before she had a chance to speak.

"I suppose your parents told you they are staying?" he said.

"Yes, but I—"

"I think it's a wonderful thing. It's just what this island needs, and now you'll never have to leave."

"Jack, I—"

He stepped further into the water, soaking them to their knees. "Feel the life in this place, Lucy?"

He released her arm and cupped his hands, bringing the salt water to his nose. "Smell it? A land unchanged by man, full of the beauty of wilderness and God's creation. How anyone can contemplate living anywhere else is a mystery."

"The island would be very crowded if no one left."

"True." He turned to face the sun setting over the horizon. "But I doubt the mainland has this view."

"Some places might. Jack," she placed a hand on his arm, "I really think—"

He put a finger over her lips. "Not yet."

"Why won't you let me speak?" She slapped the water.

"Because I don't want to hear what you're going to say." He gripped her shoulders and turned her to face him. "The words you say can never be taken back. I don't want to hear your lies because you think they are the best thing for me." He released her and ran his hands through his hair.

"Yes, I rescued you that day at the volcano, when you ran into the burning building after the kitten, and then again when you were stranded in the cave. But, Lucy, I would do it all again and many times more to keep you by my side."

She shook her head. "I've risked your life, Jack. That can't happen again. Too many people rely on you."

"So, you'd walk away and leave a hole on this island that can never be filled?"

"I think it would—"

He turned and stomped away from her,

refusing to listen to what she kept trying to say. His behavior was rude, and Anake would have his hide if she were here, but he did not want Lucy's reasons to leave to resound in his head if she left. He kicked at the water and waited for her to catch up to him.

Once she did, he led her back to the sand, where he knelt in front of her.

"Oh, no, Jack, you don't know what you're doing."

"Yes, I do." He took a deep breath. "Lucy Dillow, I love you. I love your stubbornness, your hunger for this place, your desire to do what is right. I don't mind, much, how you insist on doing what you want, even when I tell you not to."

She tried to pull away. He tightened his grip.

"But that insatiable curiosity is another thing I love about you."

"I almost got you killed, twice. You might not be so lucky a third time."

He chuckled and stood. "I'm willing to take my chances. Won't you take them with me? You're my heart, Lucy. We fought to gain your parent's approval, and now that we have, you want to walk away. If you go, I'll follow. It doesn't matter where. You can't hide from me on the far end of the world."

Tears spilled down her cheeks, the moon kissing them with silver. "You're a fool, Jack Garrison. I'll make your hair gray before your time."

"I'll look good with gray hair." He grinned.

She giggled. "Okay. Go ahead and ask me."

He fumbled in his pocket, praying he wouldn't

drop the ring in the sand. Once he had it, he focused his gaze again on her face. "Lucy Dillow, will you marry me?" He held out the solitary diamond. "This ring belonged to my mother. Will you accept it?"

She gasped. "It's beautiful. Yes, I'll marry you and wear this ring proudly." She threw her arms around his neck. "I still don't think you understand what you're undertaking."

"I think I know perfectly well." He bent his head and kissed her as the tide approached, washing the sand from their feet. He raised his head. "I want to marry you right here, in this spot, in five days. Will that be all right?"

"Why five days?"

"Your mother requested that amount of time." He kissed her again. "I think her and Anake have some preparations to do."

"So that's what they've been up to." She caressed his cheek. "Everyone seemed very sure of my answer."

"Sweetheart, your face is an open book. The entire island knew what you wanted, probably before you did yourself." He took her hand. "Do you want to go back?"

She shook her head. "Not yet. Once we do, we'll be bombarded with questions. There will be no peace ever again."

"I think I need to make building the parsonage a priority."

"Definitely," she laughed. "Unless you relish living with your in-laws."

"While your parents are growing on me, I don't think I want to live with them indefinitely." He grabbed her and kissed her again, tangling his hands in her hair. "You've made me whole."

"You've fulfilled my dreams," she whispered against his lips. "There's nothing else I could ever want."

"What about a ceremony? Children?" He traced her lips with his finger, his heart threatening to burst free and soar over the mountain. "This proposal is only the beginning. I intend to make your life wonderful."

"You already have."

17

"It's beautiful." Lucy reached out to touch the silk wedding gown, drawing her hand back before she dirtied the pristine fabric. Embroidered Hawaiian flowers dotted the skirt. The form-fitting bodice with a modest neckline was left plain, leaving the skirt and the sheer veil to take the glory.

"This is your design, Mama." Love and gratitude welled within her as she recognized the drawing from her mother's sketch. Of course, the flowers were a slight modification, and the dress contained no lace, but it still stole her breath. This was why all the secrets and the sudden desire to visit the village.

Mama nodded. "Anake heard of a shipment of white silk. We bought it all. Look." She pulled out a three foot train." It might not be practical for a beach wedding, but you'll look like a queen."

Lucy moved to the window and watched as the villagers scurried around the beach setting up chairs. On the lawn, several long tables, draped with white tablecloths, were loaded with food. After the ceremony, the Dillows would attend their very first luau. Mama and Anake had managed to combine two cultures into one wedding. In less than two hours, Lucy would wed the man of her dreams.

The five days since his proposal had fled by, leaving her mind whirling. Papa had mentioned that Jack was taking her somewhere special for a honeymoon, but everyone's lips were sealed as to where that would be. In preparation, Mama and Anake had sewed frantically to ready a new wardrobe for Lucy. One that contained day dresses, frilly nightgowns and underthings, and a gown fit for a ball.

"Move away from the window, dear," Mama said. "What if Jack sees you? It's bad luck for the groom to see the bride before the ceremony."

Lucy smiled, catching a glimpse of Jack in dress clothes as he disappeared over the rise. Was it bad luck for her to see him? She didn't think so. The time before saying their vows would drag.

"Here." Anake thrust a seaweed wrapped rice cake in her hands. "Eat. You cannot faint on such an important day."

"Thank you." Lucy kissed the woman's plump cheek. "For giving me your boy."

Anake smiled, her eyes all but disappearing in her face. "Oh, but we will share him. I could not go on without my Jack."

"Me either." Lucy took the food and perched on a straight back chair. "I want my hair loose, like a native, Mama. Not piled high and stuck with pins."

"It's your wedding." Mama stood behind her and pulled a brush through her hair with long steady strokes. "No matter how you fix it, you will be beautiful. On my wedding day, I wore my hair high, with a high lace necked gown. I felt like a princess, even more so when I saw your father in a new gray suit. It's the same suit he will wear today."

"You look very pretty in your yellow gown." Lucy glanced over her shoulder. "Like a ray of sunshine. Anake, you look like a field of tropical flowers."

She'd sewn herself a green muumuu covered with bright blossoms. "I'm as wide as a field." She patted her stomach. "But, I do like my sweets."

The three of them giggled like children as Mama continued brushing Lucy's hair and Anake made final adjustments to the veil, sewing tiny white flowers along the edge. When they'd finished, Lucy dropped her robe and stepped into the gown as Mama held it open.

The gown slid over her skin like butter. Tears pricked Lucy's eyes. She blinked them back, refusing to cry. She wanted to see Jack without a sheen of moisture obscuring her vision.

Papa poked his head into the room. "Is my princess ready?"

"As soon as Mama buttons up the back." Lucy held out the skirt. "How do I look?"

"Like an angel." He beamed, stepping forward. "I have a gift for you." He pulled a strand of pearls from his pocket.

"Oh, Papa." The traitorous tears fell. "Such an extravagance."

"Well worth the price." He moved behind her and fastened the necklace around her throat. "There.

You are complete."

"Not yet." Anake fetched the bouquet of red hibiscus and star flowers. "Now, she is ready."

~

Jack stood on the beach in new white pants and shirt, a bright red sash around his waist, and a leafy green lei around his neck. The sun was just setting over the horizon of the sea, coloring the sky with indigo, magenta, and lavender, as if God had painted the night special, just for them. Most of the village sat and waited with him for their first glimpse of the bride.

The attendees stood, obscuring his view, as a collective sigh rose. He stood on tiptoes, trying to catch a glimpse of Lucy. When she appeared on her father's arm, he swayed at her beauty. In mere minutes, she would be his as long as they both drew breath.

Her father escorted her to Jack's side, to the tune of a ukulele, before taking his place as officiate. Jack took Lucy's hands in his and stared into eyes that rivaled any star in the sky with their brilliance. He smiled, his heart racing when her lips curled.

"I thought this day would never come," she whispered.

"It took its time, but was worth the wait." He placed a kiss on her cheek.

"Let's wait for that, shall we?" Mr. Dillow said.

Those watching laughed. Lucy's face reddened.

"Dearly Beloved," Mr. Dillow opened his

Bible. "We are gathered here …"

So lost was he in Lucy's beauty that Jack needed a second prompting to respond to his vows. "I do?"

Lucy's brows raised, her shoulders shaking with silent laughter. "Is that a question?"

"No, I do. I really do."

She giggled and repeated her vows. "I do, too."

"Now, you may kiss your bride." Mr. Dillow grinned.

Jack pulled Lucy close, dipped her over his arm, and claimed her lips for the first time as her husband. It might be the first time, but he planned on doing a whole lot of kissing until the day he died. Reluctantly, he straightened, and turned to face his friends. More kisses would have to wait.

They cheered and clapped as flower petals were tossed in the path of the wedded couple. With Lucy's hand in his, Jack led her to the table designated for them. She placed her bouquet in a jar of water set there for that purpose and leaned in for another kiss as their guests took their spots.

A man in a grass skirt and beaded necklace beat on a drum, signaling several young Hawaiian girls to begin the traditional hula. Lucy gasped. "I want to learn how to do that."

"Anake will teach you. Watch what comes next."

Another man leaped into the center, twirling a flaming stick. Soon, he was joined by two more and the beating on the drum increased. Jack couldn't tear his gaze away from Lucy's enraptured expression. He would host a luau every night if it meant keeping her happy.

He fingered the pearls around her neck. "In my culture, it is bad luck to wear pearls on your wedding day. They signify tears leading to a marriage of sadness."

"Oh." She reached up to remove them.

"I am not superstitious, sweetheart. Leave them."

"Tell me more." She dropped her hands to her lap.

"See the cranes made from metallic paper?" At her nod, he continued. "There are one thousand and one. We are to display them in our home to bring luck, longevity, and prosperity. Our rings have been blessed with koa wood and ti leaves."

"I love this island." She took a deep breath. "The air is filled with the scent of flowers and roasting pork. I believe this is as close to Eden as a human could possibly get this side of heaven."

Her words warmed him. He was thrilled to know she loved his home as much as he did. With his arm around her shoulder, he sat back and enjoyed the celebration put on in their honor.

~

Lucy bit into her dinner, brought by Anake, and closed her eyes in pleasure. Imagine, an entire pig roasted underground for a full day. Delicious. Someone strummed a ukelele to provide background music. She didn't want the night to ever end.

She opened her eyes and glanced at her parents. Heads close, Mama giggled at something Papa said. What had softened her heart? Was it this place or the kindness of its people? Perhaps it was both, added to the security of Papa staying on as a permanent pastor. Mama needed stability. Uncertainty left her feeling lost.

"Are you happy?" Jack nuzzled her neck.

"More than I ever dreamed possible." She caressed his cheek, dotted with late-in-the-day stubble.

"I'll shave later, before we retire." He winked.

Her face heated. She wasn't clueless at what went on in the marriage bed, but hoped she wouldn't disappoint this man God had given her. "You'd better," she teased, shoving aside her apprehension. "You wouldn't want to mar my flawless skin."

"I wouldn't dream of it." He rubbed his cheek against hers, eliciting a shriek from her.

"Stop." She playfully shoved him back. "Let's leave and go to the beach. Let's take our first walk as husband and wife."

"What about your dress?"

"Would you mind waiting while I changed?"

He shook his head. "Just make it fast. If people suspect, we'll have a following. These wedding celebrations go on for hours."

"Be patient, my husband. I'm not going anywhere." She draped the train of her dress over her arm and hurried for the house.

Soon, dressed in a simple gown of light blue, she joined Jack in the shadows of a stand of palm trees. "How did you get away?"

"I acted as if I needed to refill my plate, then slipped around the corner of the house." He grasped her hand. Together, they raced for the water's edge.

Lucy slipped out of her white slippers and tossed them on the bank. "We should do this every night of the rest of our life."

He grabbed her around the waist, spinning her to face him. "That will be hard to do on our honeymoon, but maybe you won't mind a different beach?"

She slipped her arms around his neck. "Where are we going?"

"We're spending the night on a ship tonight and arriving tomorrow in San Francisco. I've always wanted to go there. Your parents said you've never visited."

"I haven't." She rested her cheek against his chest. "It sounds wonderful. There may still be reconstruction from the 1906 earthquake."

"We've had plenty of practice with rebuilding." His chest rumbled against her ear. "Perhaps we can give them tips."

She stared at him. "No working on our honeymoon, Mr. Garrison."

"Starting the bossiness already, Mrs. Garrison?"

"Will it do any good?"

His teeth flashed. "About as much good as it does when I tell you not to do something."

"We're in a bit of a quandary, then, aren't we?" She returned his grin. "We'll have to spend extra time working through such things."

"Will we?" He leaned down until his lips were a mere hair's length away. "Can we practice our kissing first?"

"Definitely." She pulled his head closer until their lips met. She closed her eyes and got lost in his kiss and the feel of the waves caressing her feet.

The End

Dear Reader,

The draining of the lava lake in Halemaumau happened in February of 1924. I made minor adjustments to the timeline for the sake of the story. I've also changed the names of the people involved. Still, what happened with the country's most active volcano is as close to the facts as I could find. While it is unclear as to whether the explosion at that time resulted in a lava flow or was restricted to ash and falling boulders, I took the liberty of showing the damage done by flowing rivers of fire for the sake of the story. To this time, the Kilauea Volcano is still extremely active and provides a show that attracts tourists.

The explosion of this volcano took place on the same day as the Mount St. Helen's eruption in 1980, but was thankfully, not as disastrous.

The Hanapepe Massacre was only one of several dramatic battles that shaped the relationship between labor and capital in the State of Hawaii and took place in September of 1924. I showed the first stirring of this unrest in this story.

I hope you've enjoyed this trip back in history.

Sincerely,
Cynthia Hickey

Please check out my other books at
www.cynthiahickey.com

ABOUT THE AUTHOR

Multi-published and Best-Selling author Cynthia Hickey had three cozy mysteries and two novellas published through Barbour Publishing. Her first mystery, Fudge-Laced Felonies, won first place in the inspirational category of the Great Expectations contest in 2007. Her third cozy, Chocolate-Covered Crime, received a four-star review from Romantic Times. All three cozies have been re-released as ebooks through the MacGregor Literary Agency, along with a new cozy series, all of which stay in the top 50 of Amazon's ebooks for their genre. She has several historical romances releasing in 2013, 2014, 2015 through Harlequin's Heartsong Presents, and has sold more than 260,000 copies of her works. She is active on FB, twitter, and Goodreads. She lives in Arizona with her husband, one of their seven children, two dogs and two cats. She has five grandchildren who keep her busy and tell everyone they know that "Nana is a writer". Visit her website at www.cynthiahickey.com

Printed in the USA
CPSIA information can be obtained
at www.ICGtesting.com
LVHW011358100124
768548LV00101B/5686